THE CLASH OF IMAGES

D1298438

ALSO BY ABDELFATTAH KILITO

Thou Shalt Not Speak My Language

The Author and His Doubles: Essays on Classical Arabic Culture

THE CLASH
OF IMAGES

Abdelfattah Kilito

Translated from the French by Robyn Creswell

A NEW DIRECTIONS BOOK

PROPERTY OF
SENECA COLLEGE
LIBRARIES
KING CAMPUS

WITHDRAWN

JAN 2 5 2011

Copyright © 1995 by Abdelfattah Kilito
Translation copyright © 2010 by Robyn Creswell

All rights reserved. Except for brief passages quoted in a newspaper, magazine,
radio, or television review, no part of this book may be reproduced in any form
or by any means, electronic or mechanical, including photocopying and recording, or by any information storage and retrieval system, without permission in
writing from the Publisher.

Manufactured in the United States of America
New Directions Books are printed on acid-free paper.
First published as a New Directions Paperbook (NDP1182) in 2010
Published simultaneously in Canada by Penguin Books Canada Limited

Library of Congress Cataloging-in-Publication Data

Kilito, Abdelfattah, 1945-
[Querelle des images. English]
The clash of images/Abdelfattah Kilito; translated from the French by
Robyn Creswell.
p. cm.
ISBN 978-0-8112-1886-3 (pbk.: alk. paper)
1. Boys—Morocco—Fiction. 2. Adolescence—Fiction. 3. Idols and
images—Fiction. 4. Culture conflict—Fiction. 5. Morocco—Fiction.
I. Creswell, Robyn. II. Title.
PQ3989.2.K485Q47 2010
844'.914—dc22

2010010446

10 9 8 7 6 5 4 3 2 1

New Directions Books are published for James Laughlin
by New Directions Publishing Corporation
80 Eighth Avenue, New York, NY 10011

Contents

THE CLASH OF IMAGES

We shall not cease from exploration
And the end of all our exploring
Will be to arrive where we started
And know the place for the first time.

—T. S. Eliot, "Little Gidding"

Author's Note

I'VE OFTEN ASKED MYSELF how the Arabs of long ago were able do without the image. They seem hardly to have concerned themselves with it, or at least they made no effort to propagate their own. What did Haroun al-Rashid look like? Al-Mutanabbi? Averroes? We'll never know. Of course there was, during certain periods, a knowledge of painting, but it didn't occur to anyone to have their portrait made. Our ancestors were faceless.

My idea is not at all to pity them. What I'd like to know (though this isn't the place to enter into details) is what *profit* they made by giving up figural representation. If the absence of the image is a deficiency, how did they compensate for it? A culture that proscribes the image, or that pays no attention to it—doesn't that culture invest itself elsewhere, in words, in texts, in a certain kind of literature? Perhaps it's in this light we might best study such phenomena as rhymed and metrical prose, word games, and those calligraphic techniques that attempt to make the text into a picture, to give it a *figure*.

Today everybody has a face, which is to say an image that doubles him. Everybody exists outside himself. More than that, everybody *must* have an image. An individual doesn't exist, officially, except by way of a photo ID. Wasn't the Arabs' entrance into modernity accomplished in large part thanks to the image? We're no longer alive to the scandalous side of photography, the cinema, comic strips, and illustrated books. No one, not even the fiercest critic of modernity, takes offense at them. One day perhaps we should ask ourselves what the Arabs *lost* by entering the age of the image. Because it's significant that the image imposed itself on them at the precise moment when they encountered the Other—at the moment when, coming into contact with his image, their own lost focus.

The image is to a certain extent the subject or hero of this book. The stories take place during the transition between a culture based on the text and a culture in which the image comes into being—very hesitantly at first, then more aggressively as it gains more ground—and eventually seeks to banish the text altogether, to replace it.

Each of these stories stands on its own yet they also weave a tissue of connecting threads. A certain figure reappears here and there, a certain character ("the invisible being," for example) slides more or less perceptibly from one chapter to another. Beyond that, the texts were arranged with a view toward creating a sense of continuity and significance.

A writer can't anticipate how his texts will be received. In *The Author and His Doubles* I wrote at length about al-Jahiz, the great prose writer of the ninth century. A French academic wrote to ask me if al-Jahiz had really existed, or if I had … invented him! I have to admit, I enjoyed that. To invent al-Jahiz …

Certain scenes of *The Clash of Images* have a personal, even autobiographical quality. How to deny it? At the same time, how to deal with it? To what extent am I implicated in the character named Abdallah, or in the one who says "I," or "we"? How did characters like M., the wife of R., and the fake blind man impose themselves on me, though they never existed? Life is a heap of impressions, sensations, dreams. Literature supplies a reference point, injects order into the disorder. One of the writer's tasks is to adopt a *tone*, to preserve it, and make it welcome with the reader.

Reading a story, it sometimes happens that I come across a certain passage and say to myself, "I've already lived this scene, already felt that emotion!" At such moments I have the impression that whatever I'm reading was written especially for me. It even happens that I say to myself, quite naively, "I could have written this episode, this book." In extreme cases I almost get angry with the author for having snatched away a piece of myself, for having robbed me blind! I hope my reader will recognize himself in this narrative, will approach these stories with the idea that he might have written them, and will read them as if it was indeed he who wrote them.

The Wife of R.

WHENEVER A MAN entered our street (actually a cul-de-sac that made an elbow in the middle), he would inevitably see, no matter what the hour of day, a woman's head disappearing behind a door. A stranger wouldn't pay much attention to this occurrence. At most he might experience that mild perturbation caused by the sight of a woman's face, half-concealed. He would continue on his way, without remarking that the door wasn't closed all the way, that a greedy stare pursued him, and that the head reemerged to note which house he stopped in front of. But an intimate of the place would know what was going on and with whom he was dealing. Amused or annoyed, sometimes even indignant, he would suffer the stare clinging to his back, marking the details of what he wore, gauging the weight of his shopping bag. Because the men of those days were terribly discreet, however, not one would turn around to confirm that he was being watched and confront the guilty party.

The wife of R. spent the whole day right behind her door and didn't retire into the house until night fell, just before her husband came home. She never went out and never received visitors. A woman of the threshold, she lived at the limit of the exterior world but harvested its every echo, by stealth. We knew nothing about her except that she was R.'s wife and that her curiosity knew no bounds. The neighboring women, on the rare occasions when they went out, greeted her quickly and rushed off, lest they be interrogated at length and in detail. R.'s wife would pester them with unexpected questions, stripping them bare, forcing them to reveal their most intimate thoughts. When her victims were finally able to escape, remembering that it was improper for a woman to stay out of doors so long, they returned home out of breath, with the unpleasant sense of having been shaken down and ruthlessly emptied of all their contents. It's often thought women like to tell and exchange stories but in this case the interrogations they were subjected to (and which they discussed amongst themselves, in whispers) went too far.

Seeing these women escape from the spider's web she spun behind her door, the wife of R. made do with children, to whom she would offer a pastry or some candy, and who kept her very well informed, at times even better than she hoped for. In their naiveté they said things whose full implications they didn't understand, but which opened up, for her, unexpected vistas and sudden abysses. Her eyes would go very wide when some child repeated, for example, the first words his father said to his mother on waking. Each time I returned from an errand she called me over and asked about my parents, grandparents, and cousins, sifting through my shopping bag all the while. Piece by piece she extracted information about every member of the family. And to tell the truth, I never complained, for while speaking with me she would also stroke my hair and arrange the collar of my shirt. How many secrets I gave away, all innocently!

The wife of R. had no children. When the dog from the house at the end of the cul-de-sac came out for his walk, he would pause for a moment at her door and she would run her hands gently through his fur, no doubt regretting that he hadn't been given the gift of speech.

Her husband, an exceptionally discreet man, always neat and proper, enjoyed everyone's high opinion. Children adored him because he recognized their right to play outdoors. For in fact the street didn't belong to us. As soon as someone signaled an adult's approach, we hurried back into our homes, and the street, which a moment before had rung with our shouts and games, became empty and silent as if by magic. Every adult male had authority over the children, his own as well as his neighbors', and when he surprised them in the middle of playing he would take away their little toys— marbles, jacks, or spinning tops, depending on the season. As for balls, he would plunge his nails into them and with a grimace of rage tear them all to pieces (adults, God knows why, were especially abusive toward balls). R. never disturbed us. An indulgent smile on his lips, he strolled past without breaking stride. He was getting on in years and some people muttered that he would have done better to marry a different woman. I don't know if these whisperings ever reached his ears; they would not in any case have affected his good cheer, nor would they have wiped away his disarming smile. He was the only one who didn't know his wife spent her whole day just behind the door—that's what people said anyway, pitying him all the while.

In retrospect one might imagine his wife was a victim of the social system, a system that forced her to lurk behind her own door, forced her into this wanton spying, this perversion of knowledge called curiosity. Or, in a more sophisticated fashion, one might evoke the march of History, whose sweep lies beyond the understanding of its actors: years later they discover they were the instruments of forces beyond their control, and recognize in the past clues to a logic of events they misinterpreted at the time. In this light, the wife of R. obviously prefigures the new woman, preparing to issue from her chrysalis and go boldly into the world. Her behavior is inspired by a spirit of rebellion against the bondage and ignorance that have been the lot of women. And her curiosity is evidence of the wish to educate herself, to participate in public life. At the threshold of her home, she has to take just one more step to find herself on the other side, in the territory of men. But that moment hasn't yet come.

This interpretation, plausible to a sociologist, ignores

how people saw and understood things at the time. The truth was much simpler: the wife of R. had a secret—but I should say, before giving away this secret, that basically her behavior was no different from that of historians, chroniclers, and biographers, who sift through past and present, talk to witnesses, gather confessions, and undertake long and often arduous journeys to make sure that so-and-so really did say the things attributed to him. It's true that such persons are interested in kings and viziers, exceptional individuals, while she, more modest, was only interested in an alleyway inhabited by a few families who seemed to have no history. But in her investigations she made efforts that were the equivalent of, if not greater than those made by professionals. And with the passage of years she acquired an impressive knowledge of genealogy, of alliances, antagonisms, sexual matters, dietary habits, skills and specialties, and many other things besides.

She could not, however, put her knowledge down in writing (many novelists have acquired fame by recording the acts and gestures of one street or one building's inhabitants). But as a woman who belonged entirely to the oral tradition, she never dreamed of doing so. She knew thousands of secrets, thousands of stories—she was the archivist of our cul-de-sac—yet no one came to consult her. And what good is knowledge that cannot be transmitted? Epic poetry would have been lost had the rhapsodists not recited it, circulating from town to town, and the great learning of Herodotus and al-Masudi would have vanished if they hadn't passed it down to their readers.

Inseparable from transmission, curiosity requires complicity, low whisperings, an exchange of winks: the victim is eaten completely raw, with everyone gathered around the body for a cannibal feast. The curious person is never wholly satisfied until he reveals to someone else what it is he's seen, overheard, or learned. In a strange sense, the wife of R. was an exception to this rule. She never opened up to anyone, never echoed back those sounds that reached her from the street. The ostracism she suffered meant that she didn't enjoy close ties with her neighbors. In any case, she never attempted to profit from her knowledge—by intruding, for example, in the domestic affairs of others. In fact, she was always perfectly considerate. There may even have been something contemptuous in her attitude toward others. She received all, but gave nothing. It was as if she didn't believe in the virtues of dialogue, of exchange, of sharing.

That's because she saved herself for her husband. In the evening, when he came home, she would sit at his feet and recount for him, until dawn, the stories she collected during the day. This is no doubt what explains that tolerant, vaguely amused look that R. directed at everybody and everything. Thanks to his wife's anecdotes, he was outfitted with a wisdom that rendered him serene and unflappable. You could say that she tyrannized him with the tales she served him every day, but it was a tyranny he accepted and even demanded. He needed his nightly ration of stories. When he died, we never saw his wife behind the door again.

Djinn

THE MARABOUT (what was its name, exactly?) was mostly visited by women and children. Young ones afflicted with terrible manias were brought there to have their heads knocked gently against the tomb of the saint. They were immediately cured, becoming tractable and mild. The saint had the power to calm the passions and tame the wildest tantrums, but only for children. He could do nothing for adults.

Abdallah begged Um Hani, his grandmother, to take him there. She rarely agreed. Her husband didn't tolerate her going out, certainly not to visit the tomb of a saint. And yet from time to time, on clement afternoons—afternoons of indulgence, of grace—Abdallah would find himself at the marabout, a large patio with one or two trees and a few green bushes. Children played while the women sat on gravestones and gossiped peacefully.

Abdallah was sorry not to be a madman. He tried acting like one, but his grandmother didn't believe him and assured him that, blessed as he was, he would never be anything but a model child. He did his best to act crazy, shouting and rolling around in the dust. She refused to take him seriously.

A child possessed is at the same time himself and someone else. A djinn inhabits him, holding his mind in thrall but also lending him the strength of a giant. And he is feared. People scatter from the path as he is led, kicking and foaming at the mouth, toward the saint's tomb.

What amazed Abdallah most was that moment when djinn and child separated. It was a terrible moment. A plume of smoke, at first slender, then thick, emerges from the child's head, becoming more and more dense and gradually taking the form of a djinn with flaming, torch-like eyes, a mouth as big as a cave and teeth the size of boulders. With a horrifying cry, he shakes himself off and seems about to attack the bystanders, then changes his mind and takes flight, rising into the sky where he soon becomes nothing more than a dark and tremulous speck.

The djinn's flight isn't without limits. Soaring upward, he tries to penetrate the mysteries of the heavens, the enigmas of the invisible, oracles of the future. But his curiosity is sharply reprimanded. Heaven's strong and terrible gatekeepers let fly their flaming arrows that chase the djinn away with dizzying speed. This forced retreat doesn't discourage the djinn, however. He returns to the fray and sometimes, through skillful maneuverings, manages to slip past the guardians' vigilance to seize a few scraps of forbidden knowledge. Yet this knowledge weighs him down, so he looks to parcel it out and relieve himself of its burden. He passes the knowledge on to fortunetellers, sorcerers, madmen, poets, and visionaries. And just for fun, he sometimes carries off the daughters of mortal men on their wedding night, the bride's virginity still intact.

So make no mistake—each time a shooting star streaks across the sky it is in fact a flaming arrow, shot at a djinn whose curiosity got the better of him.

At regular intervals the silence of the street was broken by voices. The raspy voice of the clay seller, arriving with his donkey from that other world, the countryside, still quite close by, only a few hundred meters from the walls of the town. The plaintive voice of the Jewish mattress repairman, who descended on people's homes with the tools of his trade, but also with his food and pots and pans. The supplicating voices of beggars, including those who made a point of stopping in front of each house and apostrophizing its inhabitants (the most peculiar was an old, dark-skinned blind man who simply demanded a roast chicken and one thousand reals—a fortune!). The thunderous voice of the secondhand clothes dealer. The nightmarish voice of a man whose profession Abdallah never quite understood, who wandered about emitting these wild syllables: "Tatap-taptataptap! Taatataptap! Hutaphutap!"

These voices are no more, replaced today by those of itinerant trinket salesmen and sidewalk peddlers. But one voice, that of the muezzin, always makes itself heard, braving time and the vicissitudes of history—gentle at dawn, aggressive at midday, lazy in the afternoon, serene at sunset, appeased in the evening.

Abdelmalek's schedule was fixed around the five daily prayers. He owned a pocket watch he only looked at to determine his ritual rendezvous with God. His grandson always went with him to mosque, except in the case of the dawn prayer.

Nevertheless, one night Abdallah woke up as his grandfather was dressing to go out and asked to accompany him. The patriarch hesitated, consulted Um Hani, and finally agreed. The two went out together. The street was dark and empty; the air was very warm. Cats howled savagely at each other. The stars glittered with such a lively, clear light that they seemed to be so close, within reach of one's hand. And the main street, when they came to it, was a marvel: lights and little street flags everywhere and not a single passerby. In this cosmic quiet and vacancy, the voice of the muezzin suddenly rang out.

Abdelmalek led the prayer in the largely empty mosque. Drops of sweat ran from his fingers and dropped to the floor mats with a dry *tick*.

On the way back home, the main street was still magnificently lit up, a magical dilapidation that went hand in hand with the extravagant potlatch of the starry sky—all for the sole benefit of Abdallah and his grandfather.

In a book called *On Those Madmen Who Are Wise*, a tenth-century writer, al-Nishaburi, remarks that the sight of a greedy man hardens the heart while the sight of a madman brings tears to the eyes.

Madmen are vagabonds. Each one feels driven to exhibit an idée fixe, to put it on display. Every day they follow the same route, indifferent to the looks of others, chasing after whatever it was that stole away their sanity.

One madman walked about swinging his head (which was ovoid) like a clock's pendulum in an uninterrupted and irritating fashion. It was said he cracked one day when forced to make a serious decision: he hesitated, but then, when pressed to make up his mind, swung his head this way and that and continued to do so ever after, even in his sleep.

Another madman, seemingly sweet-tempered and shy, never took his eyes off the street's balconies. What was he searching for? He carried a little ladder with him on his perambulations, thereby betraying a desire to climb—one he could never bring himself to realize. Perhaps he dreamed of living on a balcony, an especially good spot for peering into courtyards and discovering the intimate lives of these houses' inhabitants, down to the smallest details. This is an old dream. The demon Asmodeus amused himself at night by lifting up the roofs of homes. No secret escaped his greedy, lascivious gaze.

A third madman, who walked with his head down, carried a rucksack stuffed with obscure books. It was said that books had ruined his mind. One of the town's wise men claimed that his fault was not having studied with a master. In the past, the wise man went on, those who sought knowledge would travel long distances to meet with a master authorized to teach this or that work. Al-Tibrizi, famous commentator on the *Hamasa* and poetry of Abu Tammam, left his native Azerbaijan at an early age and traveled to Syria to study with al-Maʿarri (a blind poet of the eleventh century, who for forty years never left his home, leading an ascetic life and causing a scandal with his poetry, which was judged heretical by his most unforgiving critics). Penniless, al-Tibrizi walked on foot all the way, his only baggage the books carried on his back—which, having soaked up so much sweat, became nearly unreadable.

In contrast to these three wanderers, there was a fourth madman who chose never to leave his home, like Diogenes in his barrel or Saint Simeon on his column. He abstained from meat and lived simply on bread, olives, and figs. Holding procreation in horror, he never married. These self-imposed privations earned him the nickname of al-Maʿarri, which only half suited him since he wasn't blind. The day his mother died he attended the burial service, thereby losing the wager he made never to leave his "barrel." But what especially struck those who knew him—which is to say, everyone—was that all through the ceremony his eyes remained closed, and that he only moved about with the help of a relative. Some claimed he was feigning loss of sight, while others declared he had truly become blind.

Revolt in the Msid

SO MUCH HAS BEEN SAID—because it was necessary to say it—about the msid, that place where knowledge is acquired (for it's at the msid where children learn to read, write, and count). It was necessary to speak of it with regret, or with a fierce, retrospective indignation. Necessary to evoke the brutal instructor and the stale pedagogy he foisted on students made to learn, by heart, a sacred text they didn't understand at all. And necessary to speak, in bafflement or scorn, about the complicity of father and instructor, this one saying to that one, the first time he brings his son to the msid: "You, you kill; me, I bury." Pronounced by the father, the sentence would be carried out by the instructor. Yes, the father would authorize the instructor to beat the child to death; then he, the father, would undertake the funeral arrangements. An instructor-murderer, a father-gravedigger—the msid is the waiting room of death.

Was this murderous little speech ever spoken out loud?

Who can remember the pact that sealed his death sentence? And yet everyone knows the sentence was pronounced, must have been pronounced, even if no words escaped the father's lips. To be sure, it's only a metaphor, a hyperbole. But make no mistake, the child is guilty even if he doesn't realize it, precisely because he doesn't realize it, and must die. The msid is a stage on which a ritual murder is acted out. It is childhood—a naughty, defective, and impulsive phase—that must be put to death to prepare the way for an ontological mutation, the hazardous and necessary leap into adulthood. You don't leave the msid until you have buried your childhood.

Let's enter this storied place, of a summer afternoon. The heat inside is suffocating. Children are reciting the Quran. Facing me, facing the frail child that I was, is another child, fat and clearly miserable. His nose is covered in sweat, which he wipes off with the back of his hand. Seconds later the drops reappear and he has to wipe them off again. But there they are, beading up once more, unrelenting, in-eluctable. Fascinated, I watch and wait each time for their emergence—at first very slight, almost imperceptible, then fatter and fatter. I must have dimly perceived, in the drops' steady rhythm, in their recurrence, a fitting symbol of the msid and its daily renewal. The fat boy, exhausted by the heat, falls asleep. His body begins to lean to one side and he has to keep jerking himself upright, clawing the air, nearly waking himself up so as not to fall over. As he sleeps, he continues to wipe his nose with the back of his hand.

But the instructor is right there and doesn't miss a trick. So another drama begins (the msid is the theater par excellence). What does the instructor do? He takes a jug, fills his mouth with water and squirts it into the face of the fat boy, who wakes up—panicky and wild-eyed in the midst of our laughter—and immediately resumes his recitation of the Quran. The instructor never misses the face of a boy who falls asleep, even if he sits far away. And with the practice he gets from performing this feat several times a day, he's acquired an extraordinary skill and oral artistry.

The instructor is truly an all-powerful being, acting from a distance, without having to move. From his elevated seat he sees all, controls all, chastises without mercy. He has two canes at his disposal, a long one for collective punishments and a short one for individual beatings, usually on the soles of the feet. The oldest student, a sort of deputy in the msid, brings him the child to be punished. As long as this ordeal lasts there is a pause in the recitation. The monotony of the msid is thus interrupted, at regular intervals, by the spectacle of a beating. Although this spectacle is repetitive (it's always the same scene), each performance is new, for each student has a special way of showing his terror, crying out, contorting his body, and begging the instructor while fluttering his fingers against his mouth. Unforgettable gestures. Even when he's grown up he remains for his old friends that child who invented a novel way to suffer.

The msid's deputy is greatly envied. The instructor gives

him certain chores and in this way includes him in his secret and privileged life (for the honor of carrying to his house the basket of foodstuffs the instructor shopped for each morning, we would have killed each other). The deputy isn't merely the oldest and strongest of us, he also knows the Quran—most of it anyway—by heart. But because he lacks the infallible memory of the instructor, his knowledge of the Book must be checked on a regular basis. The instructor invites him to sit by his side and recite. And we students, awestruck, look up at these two superior beings: a god listening to and correcting a demi-god.

Memorized, the Quranic text is not, for all that, understood. You might object, but the objection would be misplaced. It assumes the Quran is, like any other book, understandable. In fact, the Word of God is by definition beyond human understanding. No one can boast of knowing it completely, not even the most seasoned and authoritative commentator. It can only be grasped partially, provisionally, and sometimes even in contradictory fashion. Only God can fathom its full meaning, its entire range of implications. It won't become wholly transparent until the end of time, when contact with the divine becomes immediate and unbroken. The Quran is bottomless—in the commentaries, what seems to be the clearest, most straightforward verse turns out to be a firecracker of unexpected connotations—so it must be learned, stored in the heart, and continuously contemplated. One must imbibe it from a tender age. To understand it means to have it inside oneself, to hold it in one's body, to make it a piece of one's life.

But let's not exaggerate the obscurity of the Quran, which introduces itself as "the clear Book." So long as one comes to it with the humility of faith, it is a miracle of lucidity. Whoever recites it, child or adult, immediately senses the rhythm of its verses, easy to recognize because unlike any other. The familiar words unveil the history of the world from beginning to end, each epoch ushered in by prophets who never cease to recall the divine law. For all of man's unhappiness arises from his tendency to forget.

And the msid is precisely where memory is cultivated, a slow, painstaking exercise that ends only with adolescence, with the awakening of sexuality, when we sever our link to childhood and bind ourselves to the community. It is by memorizing the Quran that we master the course of events, preside over the past and future of mankind, and insert ourselves into eternity.

We didn't have an actual copy of the Quran at the msid, though we all could read and write. Here, where the Word of God is so present, the Quran, as a printed text, is absent. It is on slates, and not pieces of paper, that the students write. Once the text is memorized, they wipe the slate clean and write another text in its place. One writes to make the written disappear. In the msid, the spoken word is sovereign. It is linked to the voice, to inspiration, to the soul, and to life (it is a constant theme of Arabic culture that one should gain knowledge not from books but from "the mouths of men"). The Quranic word, inseparable from its recitation, is a form of energy the believer carries with him in his body—a particle of the divine that he absorbs and mixes with his breath.

I didn't like the msid. Every day when I woke up, the prospect of going there was so terrible that I wished I were sick enough to stay in bed. But sickness rarely agreed to crawl under the covers with me, and there was no point in faking it. One morning, however, just as my grandfather was heading out, he turned to my grandmother and pronounced these winged words: "Let him stay home with you today!" An incomprehensible decision, and yet it's the nature of the divine to be both predictable and unpredictable, to establish the law, regularity, and constraint, and then, at the moment one least expects it, to break the chains, suspend the normal course of events, and introduce the miraculous into the everyday. Order would be restored starting tomorrow, no doubt. But in the meantime here was a day rescued from the monotony of the msid, a day missing from its calendar, and indeed from time itself. The child will spend this day with his grandmother, watching her mix the bread and knead the dough, forming spheres that are large and soft, like breasts swollen with milk—breasts she then pounds flat, leaving the impress of her fingers.

History marched on and one incident, whose full implications were beyond the grasp of my peers and I, revealed, albeit indistinctly, the flaw of the msid. One day the instructor struck the student Fa, and Fa protested. He didn't cry, didn't beg for mercy, didn't play the customary role of the student in such situations. Instead of adopting a posture of fear and submission, he stood up to the instructor. It was the only show of revolt I saw during my entire time at the msid. In retrospect I feel great admiration for Fa, but at the time his behavior could only shock me and my peers. He was asking for something unheard of: teaching without violence. For the first time, the legitimacy of the msid beatings was challenged, which meant a challenge to the power of the instructor, the power of the father—and, in this way, an entire educational system, an entire social structure.

Faced with this rebellion, the teacher showed himself capable of exceptional violence (four students held Fa still while the blows rained down on him). But a glint of worry and fear suddenly flashed from his eye. In order to save face and maintain his authority, he'd been forced to become even more brutal. Overcome with pain, Fa finally did cry, but his tears were of anger and fury. We were disappointed the instructor hadn't been able to subdue him, to tear from him the acknowledgment of his wrongdoing. We wanted him to beat Fa again, to wipe out his opposition to the msid and its regime, to batter down his wicked revolt. We wanted the instructor to kill him.

Today it's hard for me to explain this feeling of solidarity with the instructor. Was it cowardice, a desire to be on the side of the oppressor, the magnetism of the executioner?

Was it fear of chaos, the inability to imagine a system different from that of the msid? Or was it some dark jealousy I felt toward Fa, that puny boy with frail health, inept at sports and fisticuffs, who had suddenly shown unexpected nerve, who had gone head to head with the instructor and dared to do what all of us, in some buried part of ourselves, would have liked to dare to do? No, there was another reason. At the msid we had been ingrained with a story from the beginning of time, from the moment of Adam's creation: the story of Satan's revolt. Fa was reenacting the insubordination and pride of the angel created from fire, who refused to prostrate himself before a being created from clay. We were witnessing a revival of that drama in which the first human, backed by divine favor, opens his astonished eyes onto the world of things. Confronted by such a spectacle we had no other choice but to stand with God, just as the assembly of angels did in the original performance.

Satan found himself alone, utterly alone. Later on in his going to and fro, he seduced Adam and Eve, and then their descendents, except for a small number who remained faithful to God. So Satan was able to turn the tables: alone at the outset, he finished with a host of disciples.

Fa continued to attend the msid. We shunned him. Then one day he didn't show up and we learned that he had gone to school with the French, the Infidels. Few could resist the tempter's appeal. One after another, we followed Fa. The msid emptied and the instructor saw a day coming when only he would remain. But then the righteous man is always alone.

I've kept only a vague memory of the drama that erupted at home between my father and my grandfather, of which I was the inadvertent cause. They were talking about me, discussing whether to send me among that mythical people, the French. Bursts of shouting were followed by heavy silences. My grandmother, past master in the art of supporting her son without opposing her husband, got very upset, sometimes shouting louder than the two men. From the foot of Olympia I watched this irruption of the numen while pretending to be busily at play. A mortal has every reason to be anxious when he is the subject of a quarrel between the gods.

My grandfather yielded, reluctantly, and I went among the Infidels. A week or two later, while I was engaged in deciphering a book, I heard him say to my grandmother softly: "The boy has learned French." His tone was serene, indulgent, even pleased. Had the patriarch abandoned his principles? Had the winds of history swept him up, too? Or had he bowed to God's omnipotent will? Had he understood that success in the modern world requires an apprenticeship in the language of the Infidels? Or had he felt a kind of pride seeing that his grandson knew a language he didn't, and never would (since he had no use for it)? Had he felt a sudden surge of sympathy for this child lost in a forest of foreign symbols?

I incline toward a different explanation: the patriarch had arrived at the abrupt realization that the conflicts dividing the world are caused by men, by history, and not by languages as such—that French, like Arabic, is essentially a system of sounds and letters, a game with rules of grammar and syntax, and that in this sense all languages are equal, since each is a gift from God.

When I asked him to tell me what God was like, to describe His face for me, my grandfather smiled and, perceiving that I was in danger of becoming lost in a labyrinth of theological debates, simply answered me with a citation from the Quran: "Nothing resembles Him. He is All-Hearing, All-Seeing."

On Friday afternoons the instructor took us with him to the cemetery. We were happy, because we knew that after reciting a few Quranic verses for the dead our reward would be a plate of couscous, a plate that would appear out of nowhere, delivered by some charitable soul, or rather an angel dropping from the sky. This God-blessèd couscous, this couscous wolfed down amidst the gravestones—oh, it was tasty! "Said Jesus son of Mary: 'O God our Lord, send down upon us a table from heaven, and it shall be a feast-day for first and last among us, and a miracle from You, and grant us your bounty—You are the best of providers.'"

It was a holiday and so the rules of the msid were suspended. The instructor, a far off look in his eyes (no doubt he was thinking of his dear departed), allowed us to frolic and run through the bitter perfume of herbs and wildflowers. The sea glittered close by. On the wall of a holy man's tomb the rain had flaked away the lime and traced a shape, wherein I found a face—an immense face, with vague contours—but I told no one of my discovery.

•

The instructor became an old man. Sick and weak, he wanted to visit the holy places before he died, wanted to drink the water of Zamzam, throw stones at Satan, circle the Ka'aba, and see the tomb of the prophet. But for this he would need a passport and therefore—horror of horrors— a photograph.

He was full of contempt for images and especially for photography, a diabolical invention that mimicked creation and competed with the work of God. The sky, the earth, the sea, the beasts, mankind and all the infinite variety of the world emerge from this black box, just as they emerged at the beginning of time from the will of God. The Seducer, Master of Illusion, fabricates a second genesis in black and white, all surface, cold and flat as a mirror—a mirror all the more dangerous for being perfectly accurate. "Yes, but let them try putting a soul in it," he would say in vengeful tones. Photography was a hoax, a vain copy, an insidious re- flection and satanic artifice, showing water where there was only a mirage, life where there was only death. "Anyone who gives himself up to photography allies himself with the enemy of mankind and sins against God."

Nevertheless, he had to hand his image over to the Se- ducer; to fulfill a religious duty, he had to break the pro- hibition of images. Perhaps this explains the look of great sadness that he flings, even today, at all those who raise their eyes to his image, in the house where he no longer lives.

His son accompanied him to Casablanca, where he was to catch the boat. On the quay they met three of his old students, now grown up, who were also going to Mecca. As soon as they saw him they ran toward him, joyfully, and because he was hardly able to walk they carried him all the way to the boat. The son gave them a purse with funds for the voyage.

Two months later he came back, still carried by his students. He was even feebler than when he left. The students returned the purse, unopened. They had paid all the instructor's expenses. For two months they had cared for him, bathed him, fed him from their own hands. It was on their shoulders that he performed the rites of pilgrimage.

The Sparrow

AS A CHILD, ABDALLAH believed that doctors did not eat.
They had no need to consume meat and vegetables, to sip
tea and coffee, for they knew the secrets of life and death.
They even turned their noses up at milk and the sweetness
of pastries. They inhabited a place apart, beyond the reach
of time (they had surely drunk from the fountain of youth).
Visiting a sick person, they seem to arrive by magic, angels
of the moment, anxious to return to that heaven from which
they are descended. Although they look human, they speak
a foreign language and the brief, beguiling words they pro-
nounce are transformed on paper into spells and cabalistic
formulae. Why eat, when thanks to an occult and effica-
cious science, they know how to summon strength and well-
being, fight off death, perform miracles? From time to time,
just to get by, they casually imbibe some bitter compound,
or sip on a vial of sweet and fruity liquid, like the gods of
Olympus who live on nectar and ambrosia; or like the saints

who, attempting to rise above the human condition, eat only grass (like sheep) or else, after the manner of angels, fast continuously, allowing themselves at most one date or raisin per day. In this rigid diet lies the secret of the saints' power, their thaumaturgy. They have only to lay their hands on a sick person and he is healed at once.

Old Abdelmalek was skeptical of saints, whose exploits, whenever they were recounted to him, never caused more than a furrowed brow or contemptuous frown. As for doctors, all of them "Nazarenes," he stubbornly refused to have anything to do with them. He claimed that if there were no doctors there would be fewer sick people. One should rely on oneself and avoid excess, the source of all evils (on this point, without knowing it, he was a Platonist). In any case, he took care never to fall ill.

Death was something Abdelmalek saw every day, a familiar occurrence. People didn't die in a hospital (there was no such thing) but at home, surrounded by relatives. Death preyed on infants in particular; every day one saw their little bodies being carried to the cemetery, wrapped in sheepskin blankets. Abdelmalek lost three boys, all of whom he had named Muhammed. To master his grief after each death he must have found it necessary to recall the example of the Prophet, that most virtuous of men, whose male children all died young.

Abdelmalek's steadfastness and faith were rewarded: his last male child survived the measles. He, too, was named Muhammed, for in Abdelmalek's mind this unhoped-for son was a copy, reproduction, or resurrection of his brothers. He was a reminder of them and a remembrance. They had passed away at the ages of five, three, and one, respectively. Nor would they ever grow up. In paradise they would remain the same age as when they died, and would have all eternity to play at marbles and jacks.

One summer evening Abdelmalek went to join them in the Garden. He had collapsed three days before his death, and because he was unconscious it was permitted to call a doctor (at the time one didn't visit the doctor, it was he who made visits, usually when the patient was on the verge of death). Head lowered, the doctor announced himself and went into the patriarch's room. He came out almost immediately and then, his head still lowered, left the house. Abdelmalek died the next day. He was right, there was no use calling a doctor. He was attended instead by that angel who escorts human souls to their natural end, and who, moved by a strange pity, granted this faithful servant of God one more night before the end.

During the funeral observances a large crowd filled the house. Young Abdallah was lost among the unfamiliar faces; no one paid him any attention except his grandmother, who gave him a difficult mission. Passing him a handkerchief and looking at him tenderly, she said, "To wipe away your tears." But he hadn't been crying, and felt no need to. The handkerchief reminded him that nevertheless he must shed a few tears, that it would be improper for him to remain dry-eyed. He felt all the more guilty since surrounding him were nothing but mournful looks and reddened eyelids. In the kitchen two fat women were gulping down hard-boiled eggs. His grandmother returned to the attack: "Go pay respects to your grandfather." The corpse was covered up to the neck in a white sheet (was this the shroud?). "Kiss him," she commanded. Abdallah bent over and brushed his lips against a brow as smooth and cold as marble.

When they returned from the cemetery they ate bread, butter, and honey. Everyone moved about slowly and spoke softly, as if not wanting to disturb the soul of the deceased, floating up among the recesses of the home. In the evening, tongues loosened. The guests delivered their funereal orations for Abdelmalek, each in his own fashion, and by dinner they had moved on to other subjects—at first shyly, then boisterously, calling out to one another from table to table. Suddenly, a burst of laughter, clear and piercing. There was a moment of uncertainty, then the laughter bubbled up again and this time, by some mysterious and lighting-fast contagion, it spread everywhere, powerful, irrepressible, uninterrupted, with male and female modulations and the entire range of individual tones. It lasted until dawn and then gradually lost force, like a storm moving off into the distance. Everyone sank into sleep.

Only Um Hani remained standing, busying herself at the stove to make the soup. In the majestic calm of the early morning a chirping sound came from the courtyard and a sparrow hopped into the kitchen. He approached the grandmother and, fixing his eye on her, continued chirping.

The old woman's nose began to tremble (a sign, as Abdallah well knew, of some great emotion) and a fat tear rolled down her cheek. Throughout the period of mourning the bird came early each day to keep her company. After the fortieth day, he vanished.

The dead are good "transmitters" of stories. One begins by weeping over their absence, by speaking to them, apostrophizing them, even scolding them for having abandoned their relatives to so much grief. Afterward, one tells how they passed away to those who don't yet know—who have come, as they say, to offer condolences. The story of the dead man's last moments is in this way built up piece by piece; each visitor has the right to a small, dry scrap of story, composed simply of facts reported with utter objectivity. The commentaries—prolix, teeming, infinite—don't come until later. Each visitor brings his own memory, each relates that biographical detail he himself witnessed, or knows by hearsay. So, little by little, a novel is built out of many voices, a hagiography composed of anecdotes, witticisms, character traits, a long list of virtues, good deeds, and unsuspected talents that no one would think of disputing. Piously arranged, the novel keeps evolving as long as it continues to be transmitted.

But eventually one notes with consternation that the novel is getting thinner, falling apart, flaking away. In place of that wealth of incidents, that luxuriance of scenes and tableaux, only a few stereotypical episodes are left, languishing and wasting away. Inversely, the dead man's tomb, though neglected, is covered by a wild growth, thick and abundant, which obscures even the marble slab where his name is engraved.

Loss of name is what the dead fear most. Deprived of their bodies, mere phantoms of themselves, they're also stripped of their biographies, which survive only in fragments. Questioned by a traveler lost in the next life, the dead have only one story left to tell: the story of the moment that decided their fate and assigned them their place in the hereafter. This story is a distillation of their whole life, a story that is distilled in turn by their name—which, as they know, might easily fade away and cease to signify anything. In Purgatory, the gentle, unfortunate Pia says to Dante: "Remember me: I once was Pia!"

A Glass of Milk

ABDALLAH HAD THE RIGHT every morning to half a glass of milk, no more. His mother, who wouldn't bend on this point, nevertheless allowed him to fill his glass to the top with water, a compromise he agreed to. Abhorring a vacuum, he enjoyed self-deception.

Monsieur Nourrissier, the principal, stood at the door of the school from 7:30 on, an iron ruler in hand. The instrument was a veiled threat—never carried out—and an emblem of power, a scepter. In the apartment above the school, his son, then four years old, sat every morning by the window watching the students with his wide blue eyes. He held a bottle of milk in his hands, which he often forgot to raise to his lips. It was a big bottle, all for him, an enormous glass whose equal Abdallah had never seen at home or anywhere else. Abdallah's friend Ali, nicknamed Fats, claimed that the principal's son lived exclusively on milk, either as a special privilege or because, being pink-skinned and blond, he was made of different stuff than they were.

Wide-eyed at his high window, half-empty bottle in hand, he watched the little Arab boys shouting, laughing, and jostling each other on their way toward the school door. A child's mind being what it is, he must have wished to be what they were, must have felt shut out, must have wished to look like them, dress like them, and play their games.

Without moving from the window frame, he grew up.

Scene change: a teenager now, the boy has become a comic book hero, Miki the Ranger. He's no longer blond but still drinks milk and nothing but milk. (Miki. *Milk*.) This is no doubt the reason for his glow of well-being, the shine of his skin, his forthright stare. In a single bound he leaps astride his horse and chases after redskins and bandits. When he shoots, he always hits the bulls-eye. His exploits earn him the love of Susie (is that her name?), a girl with clear, awestruck eyes and a rosy face, always smiling except when she's jealous, which only happens on the heels of some trivial misunderstanding, naturally. Miki the Ranger is a lucky fellow. He goes from success to success, never knowing doubt or despair.

He is seconded on his adventures by Double Rum and Professor Bloodletter, tireless companions, devoted and true, but also notorious boozers, bearing on their faces the stigmata of their vice—the little red lash-marks of alcoholism. Double Rum is a small man, unkempt, with wrinkled and vicious eyes, dry lips, and a patchy beard (not to be confused with the well-trimmed beard of the bandit chief).

Professor Bloodletter is a big man with badly shaven, hollow cheeks and deep-set, languorous eyes, quick to take offense or suffer a reproach. Two ridiculous and predictable characters, loyal only to Miki and themselves, always on the sniff for rum and forever digging themselves into holes they can't get out of. But beardless Miki, drinker of milk, Miki the Pure, arrives just in time to rescue them.

If milk is the secret of Miki's powers, of his superiority to the imbibers of alcohol, it's also what sets him apart and excludes him, in a certain sense, from his community. Miki is the only milk drinker of the Wild West. Milk is his sin, his shame. Here's a typical scene: Miki enters a crowded saloon and politely orders a glass of milk. All the cowboys burst out laughing. One of them, the fattest, sidles up to him and treats him as if he's a baby. Bent over with laughter, he asks if Miki wouldn't like his mother's tit, pretends that he's about to go look for it, and then, changing his mind, decides to wean the boy by making him drink a glass of whiskey. Miki, features thrown into a rage, lands a straight jab to the chin. The man goes down in a heap but another cowboy leaps to the attack. Double Rum and Bloodletter, already quite cockeyed, wade into the fray on shaky legs and soon the saloon is a battlefield. In the end, Miki leaves without having drunk his milk. Justice was on his side (the results of the brawl confirm as much), but he's flustered and his face has lost its usual milky serenity. His triumph has a bitter taste. He hasn't been fighting outlaws, just some regulars relaxing at the saloon after a hard day's work. And yet, in each man's features he discerned all the pettiness and villainy of which humans are capable. For a long time Miki will keep aloof, asking himself whether the company of bandits isn't preferable to that of these upright citizens, who treat him so unmercifully, with such inhumanity.

In a sense, he is the cause of this scandal. His error is to insist at all costs on his distinction from everyone else, even his companions. Each time he enters a bar he has to fight his anxiety, take up arms against conformism and peer pressure. Miki pays a steep price for this attachment to his favorite beverage. Even before ordering he knows they will mock him, knows he will observe the same repulsive laughter on the same vulgar faces—but he also knows that he'll hit back, defending his right to milk with his fists. After all, he doesn't want to lose his soul, the true source of his powers. So he leaps to the defense of his childhood and fights to keep it safe—and forever remains the little blue-eyed boy who, from his window above the school, observes the students' fun while drinking from his bottle of milk.

One afternoon Abdallah went to visit his mother. He felt tired, discouraged. She saw as much at a glance, but had long resigned herself to his not sharing with her his deepest thoughts and concerns. They talked listlessly of this and that. Abdallah's mind was elsewhere. He was worrying over something, exactly what he couldn't say, but it kept him from taking an interest in anything but himself. All at once he spotted a comic book, a new issue of *Kiwi*, lying abandoned on the sofa. On its cover the intrepid Blek le Roc, knife in hand, fought with a black bear in the middle of a forested landscape. Zhor left to prepare the tea, knowing that her son's single-minded passion for images would make her own presence unnecessary for a little while.

Abdallah was surprised to see that *Kiwi*, a comic he'd read some thirty years ago, was still being published. He began reading with the same pleasure and enthusiasm as before. He was vaguely aware of his mother in the kitchen, clinking cups and spoons; then he sensed her coming close, placing a cup of tea in front of him. He sensed that she had returned to her seat and was folding laundry. But she was only shadow now, less real than these three old friends, fighting for the independence of the American colonies: Blek le Roc, in his thirties, Roddy (eight years old? ten?), and Professor Occultis, in his fifties. Curling up on his side and turning away from his mother, who continued to fold the laundry in silence, Abdallah regressed into childhood. Reading, he became a boy of ten again, deaf and blind to the world around him. He knew he was ignoring his mother, preferring the company of these paper beings to hers. A familiar feeling of guilt. Most of his time as a child was spent looking at pictures instead of doing his homework.

Closing *Kiwi*, Abdallah sat back up. To read a comic book is to lean over, be drawn downward, plunge into the well of oneself at the risk of disappearing, forever, into the waters of that magical pond. Rejoining the real world, Abdallah turned toward his mother. She looked tired to him, older. She always maintained such a serene demeanor, seeming to float above life's tribulations—but what did he know? What dreams, what hopes had she been forced to renounce? At the price of what effort, what struggles, had she won this calm and even-temperedness? She didn't know the doctors had already passed their sentence: "Six months, a year, maybe two ..."

Feeling that she was being observed, his mother began talking of trivial things so as to avoid the essential, the time that was passing, the death that waited, and the fragility of this instant, in which they both remained hopelessly silent. Abdallah thought of Blek and Roddy and Occultis— happy, radiant, without secrets, absorbed entirely in their adventure—and suddenly realized that they hadn't grown any older. Time had no power over them. Thirty years had passed and they remained the same age, with the same faces, the same bodies. Their world, for all its surface agitation, remained frozen and still. Captives of a single moment in the history of the United States, they could never evolve, advance, or change. They had no future, nor any past. Appearing for the first time, they already were what they always would be: the same features, same personality, same adventure. Alongside the trappers, the "patriots," they would fight forever, unrelentingly, against the British Redcoats (also known as lobsterbacks). In the meantime, their creator grows old, and one day he'll die. But there is no reason why they themselves should cease to exist. They'll always remain true to their age, which will never change, and they'll always fight for the independence of the American colonies, which will never be achieved.

They'll also keep the same costumes. In *Tintin and the Picaros*, the last book of the series, Tintin wears a pair of straight trousers rather than his famous plus fours, as essential to his character as the upswept quiff. He's older. One could guess his age, although in previous books one never quite knew if he was a child or an adolescent. By changing his pants he suddenly becomes a modern, well-adjusted young man, sporting the styles of his day. He's no longer truly Tintin. He's lost a piece of his soul.

"Drink your milk," Zhor says. Abdallah now sees that it wasn't a cup of tea she had placed before him, but a glass of milk. It was exasperating; not only had his mother intuited how tired he was (though this was no longer the case), but she also provided the remedy, a rejuvenating glass of warm, sweetened milk. And this was of course what he had sought that day, coming to visit her—but he refused to acknowledge it just then, out of shame, or vain stubbornness.

The Image of the Prophet

ONE MORNING, A WOODEN BOX, placed atop a small table, caused quite a stir among the neighborhood children.
After paying a couple of sous, you could look through a
hole into the interior. There you saw an image, and then
another, which quickly gave way to a third. A dozen images passed by in this way, set in motion by a piece of string
twirled by the box's proprietor, a man who puffed peacefully on his cigarette, indifferent to the tumult he had created. I remember nothing of the show itself; the images
passed by quickly, too quickly for me to seize their pattern.
A magical, multicolored world was unveiled—a beauty lost
as soon as looked at.

I had never seen any images properly speaking, except
my own in the mirror. On the walls of our house there
were no photographs, no reproductions of any sort. The
walls were white, cold, and smooth, with no more than one
Quranic verse in calligraphy: "The All-Merciful is seated

firmly upon the throne." An ambiguous verse and one
that—despite the ingenuity of exegetes bent on removing
all traces of anthropomorphism—*presents an image* (Arab
theologians needed several centuries to quell the tendency
to lend divinity a human form).

It was only once I learned to read that I was actually able
to decipher images.

There were a number of these, images with a certain
prestige, sold not far from the great mosque. Each told a
story, or else the climactic moment of a story, with a religious subject. Ali, the fourth caliph, was especially promi-
nent. In one image he is seen seated, a saber across his legs,
flanked by his sons Hassan and Hussein, and with a couch-
ant lion close by. In another he is on horseback confronting
an infidel knight, whom he has just split in two with his saber, crown to belly. In a third his adversary, still living, holds
a broadsword in one hand and, in the other, his own left
arm, which he has just lost and still gushes blood. He seems
to look at the spectator standing outside the scene and appeal to him as a witness to the atrocity of his suffering. In
others I recognized a number of prophets: Noah in his
ark, with full menagerie; Solomon among his servants, several of whom are djinn, identifiable by their wicked mein
and assortment of tails, hooves, and horns; Abraham, sup-
plied with a beard that reaches to his knees, is about to slit
the throat of his blindfolded son, but the angel is already
there bearing the sacrificial ram (curiously, the angel has
long hair, breasts, and feminine features). Under a tree en-

twined by the serpent, Adam looks at Eve, who leans over
and lends an ear to the poisonous conspirator, the serpent's
forked tongue flickering with menace.

These were considered edifying images that exalted the
faith and exemplary figures of the past, though at the cost
of violating the ban on figural representation. One limit
was respected, however: the prophet of Islam was never
pictured. The prophet was a story, a word in the mouth,
not a face. And yet many claimed to have seen him in their
dreams (with what features?).

In a middle school reader, designed by French educators
for Moroccan students, there was a text that recounted the
prophet's flight from Mecca to Medina. I was astonished
that non-Muslims knew of the Hegira, the founding moment of Islam and keystone for the new history. So the
Event was recognized and corroborated by Christians. In
my naiveté this struck me as all the more remarkable, since
I didn't imagine a scene from the life of Christ would figure in any Arabic reader.

The text was accompanied by an image. In the back-
ground, several horsemen reined in their mounts, which
reared up with impatience. These were the unconverted
Meccans, who had rushed into the desert in pursuit of the
Prophet. Their horses must have sensed a human presence,
and indeed, in the foreground, a man hid behind a rock. He
wore a turban, a checkered jalabiya, and a flat leather sack
strung across his chest. A short, trim beard covered his jaw.

There was no doubt about it: he was the Prophet.

This was, on the part of the illustrator, a risky undertaking, and one whose full consequences he didn't seem to have considered—unless, knowing the students who made up his audience were rather provincial, he was simply defying a prohibition he felt to be unjustified. And of course he could have invoked (supposing he was familiar with them) those miniatures from the Turkish manuscript that illustrate the Night Voyage and Ascension of the Prophet—miniatures that show him journeying through celestial expanses on the back of a winged horse, and during the various stages of his heavenly exploration. Just as the Turkish miniaturist gave the Prophet features that belonged to the local artistic tradition, the illustrator of our textbook had lent him the appearance of a Moroccan peasant—and this was perhaps what troubled me the most, having been raised, like my peers, with a town-dweller's traditional disdain for the peasantry.

The illustrator, however, had no reason to hold peasants in disdain. The country life must have meant, for him, liberty, excitement, adventure. Perhaps he had taught in some remote village, way up in the mountains; perhaps he had shared in the life of the shepherds and workers, drunk their sweet tea, eaten couscous flavored with rancid butter, traveled on the back of a mule, and stammered out a few words of Berber or Arabic; perhaps he even accustomed himself, sweet agony, to sit on the ground Indian-style. What else could he do in his illustrations but reproduce what he saw around him? Though its subject was an episode from the life of the Prophet, the image, when you looked closely at its details, actually revealed the vision of the illustrator. Lacking an Arab life model customarily used for inspiration, he gave the Prophet the appearance of an ideal peasant. Instead of that patriarchal, bristly, and electric beard of the biblical prophets, "Muhammed" had a short, boxed beard, neatly groomed. He looked, on the whole, quite elegant and distinguished.

And yet, was it by accident that the illustrator had chosen to depict him at the moment he was ducking for cover? Crouched behind the rock, he watches his pursuers furtively—though they do not notice him at all, lost as they are in the desert labyrinth of their impiety. He watches them out of one eye only, to make sure they haven't spotted him. The image is a site where eyes flee from each other, where glances never meet, where there is no face-to-face or actual encounter. The unbelievers don't look toward the place where the man they chase is hidden. And as for the reader, he can't distinguish all the features of the Prophet, who is drawn only in profile. Indeed, it's as if the illustrator—by half-concealing his body, by hiding him and preventing any face-to-face with the reader—sought a compromise with the ban on representation.

In class, there was no discussion of this image and the text was neither read nor remarked on by Monsieur Andet, who probably felt it would be out of place for him to teach a subject belonging to a faith and tradition unfamiliar to him. With this decision, he had, in his own way, also censured the image of the Prophet. The students didn't seem to notice the picture. They didn't see it, or at least they never talked about it—the subject was taboo.

I found myself bearing a heavy secret, and my grandfather was no longer there for me to unburden myself. In any case, he would have shielded his face from this sacrilegious image and experienced, alongside his impotent rage, a bitter satisfaction: "I told you a thousand times the French school would teach nothing but impiety. No one wanted to listen to me. This is what you get." I went to my grandmother, a last recourse. And in her usual custom of looking at an image, she joined thumb to index finger, then held this makeshift monocle against her right eye. She examined the image for a long time, in silence. But it seems that she saw nothing, or that she saw something else entirely.

Don Quixote's Niece

AFTER THEIR WEEKLY VISIT the cousins sometimes left behind their books, illustrated novels that Abdallah would leaf through without actually reading them. He sounded out words and phrases but they had no meaning for him, and the images remained mute, far off, as if saddened at not being able to convey their urgent, vital message. A vague fear paralyzed Abdallah. He worried that reading would unlock dreadful secrets, or bestow an unmerited gift. Many people never get past this first hurdle. They study hard, become competent professionals, write first-class reports, play with ideas, and yet remain unable to read a literary text. Or they simply don't dare. A terrible voice, a voice they obey their whole life, forbids them from opening books. So a novel or collection of poems becomes for them a quasi-magical object, a store of esoteric knowledge, off-limits to the layman. The origin of this attitude is no doubt that fear inspired by the scholarly tome, studied with veneration under the guidance of an all-powerful teacher, an authorized exegete, meaning's licensed middleman (the poet Shawqi wasn't wrong in comparing him to a prophet). Without his intercession one might read the text awry and so slip into heresy.

Quest for Fire was the first novel that fell into Abdallah's hands, a large volume with red cardboard covers and black-and-white illustrations of half-naked men and women, a hugely yawning lion, and a giant elephant (actually a mammoth) caressing with the tip of his trunk a man with his head bowed—a man whose name was Noah, but who had nothing in common with the biblical character. Nightmare images that suggested a story all the more terrifying because the succession of pictures didn't add up to anything coherent. Abdallah had no better luck with *The Prince and the Pauper*, though it was beautifully illustrated in color: a rustic cabin, a chateau, sad-faced peasants, men and women in extravagant costumes, and two children who looked exactly alike, only distinguishable by their manner of dress. The words refused to disclose the wonderful world that Abdallah suspected lay behind them. There was a grand party at the chateau, to which he was not invited. He stood outside, eyes fixed on the imposing gate, through which slipped an occasional strain of music, waft of perfume, or burst of laughter. He was sure he'd never be one of the elect, descending from their carriage and making their way toward the festivities between ranks of bowing, uniformed servants. Abdallah was very sad. It was a time in his life when he despaired of learning to swim and fell off, pathetically, every time he tried to get on a bicycle.

But one day he gained entrance to the forbidden chateau by way of a trapdoor: the comic book. *Kiwi, Rodeo*— what pleasure! A new continent arose before his astonished eyes. A young Columbus, he set foot on land all the more blessed for never having been promised.

This novel pleasure was nevertheless accompanied by a certain anxiety. Throughout the course of the story the reader was drawn toward whatever lay ahead—the outcome of a battle, for example, or the solution to some puzzle— but this feverish curiosity led, inevitably, to the end of the tale. An end both desired and feared, for by reestablishing an order that had been threatened, by returning things to their proper places, it cast the reader back into his own world. He wound up once again in that familiar universe, necessarily banal and degraded by comparison with the heroic one that had just been revealed to him: "End of episode."

But the most painful thing was to discover that the last pages had been ripped out by some sacrilegious hand (that the first pages should be missing was no great loss as the story repeated itself often enough), or else, although it amounted to practically the same thing, that fatal "to be continued" fell on the story like the blade of a guillotine— at a moment of extreme tension, of course, with the hero in a perilous fix, desperately fighting an enemy with superior numbers. "To be continued": a promise that is in fact a threat, or warning. With this sentence the reader is arbitrarily and ignominiously expelled from a world where he was perfectly at home. Having committed no crime he's punished by an impersonal decree without appeal. In the end it's he and not the hero (certainly capable of looking after himself), who finds himself in a desperate fix.

In the world of the comic strip and the adventure story the most common reflex is to put up one's guard, protect oneself, circle the wagons, beat a retreat inside the fort, behind a tree trunk, or up to some high place of refuge. The action takes place in enormous forests, vast deserts, and wide-open prairies, but the actors—instead of each confining himself to a portion of this space—converge on the same spot, making confrontation inevitable. After the hecatomb, the survivors separate and scatter across the face of the earth, like the first peoples after the fall of Babel.

To take refuge is also a reflex of the reader, who ensconces himself in the deepest recesses of his house, climbs up into the attic, or slips into bed (which one author has happily compared to an island). But despite his precautions, the world he has set aside remembers him and harasses him. He's forced time and again to abandon his beloved heroes to open the door for visitors, to run an errand, to eat, and above all to do his homework, to learn his lessons. In school, he listens distractedly to the instructor. His mind is elsewhere, among the plains and forests of America, where redskins and settlers attack each other without respite. His mother begins to worry. Reading is bad for his eyes and health; it also addles the brain. His father begins to doubt whether there's any connection between reading picture books and a future career as a doctor. He says nothing, but his look of disapproval shows he's looking for an excuse to take action. He finds one in the boy's report card. The grades are disastrous, except for Dictation; he breaks into a violent rage and formally prohibits his son from reading comic books.

Books can kill; they can also cause madness. This is what literature, long before Cervantes, never ceases to make clear. Books are wicked. But this claim, in order to be formulated, paradoxically needs the support of another book—this one supposedly innocent, or benign.

The danger comes not only from chivalric romances, but from all novels, no matter what their genre. Forced into a year's retirement from his career as a knight, Don Quixote plans to lead the idyllic life of a shepherd, which is to say, to live in accordance with the conventions of the pastoral novel. Whenever one genre falls into disfavor another immediately replaces it. On his deathbed, Quixote recovers his sanity for a moment to say, "It only grieves me that this destruction of my illusions has come so late that it leaves me no time to make some amends by reading other books that might be a light to my soul." What books? Books of religious edification no doubt, detailing the lives and deeds of the saints. To atone or to repent is necessarily to fall into another form of madness, a new kind of playacting. Don Quixote wants to retreat into the desert and take up the life of a hermit. He aspires to sainthood. Only death prevents his setting out on this new career—one that would be prompted, like the previous one, by literature. We know that Saint Teresa of Avila wrote a chivalric romance before turning toward mysticism. Her vocation, according to her biographer Father Ribera, had its origins in her reading of hagiographic tales: "The heart of young Teresa was set aflame with stories of the sufferings and deaths of martyrs ... and she soon began yearning to die as they had, in order to earn the crown they had won. This yearning was so ardent that she finally left the house of her father, along with her brother, taking only a few provisions, both of them determined to seek out the land of the Moors, where they would lose their heads for the love of Jesus Christ." Doña Teresa, Saint Quixote.

Must books be burned? Yes, the hidalgo's niece responds without hesitation, motivated by an implacable hatred toward the romances that have corrupted her beloved uncle's mind. By making them endure the torments of fire "like so many heretics," she aims to eliminate evil. But this is a vain undertaking. Don Quixote has already read everything, and in any case his reading days are over. The life he seeks to lead, beginning with his first adventure, is the life of a knight-errant; he wants to change the world, and the loss of his books will in no way divert him from this goal. The evil is already done, and the niece knows it. If she rails so passionately against books, if she incites the curé to destroy them, it's because she imagines they exercise a malefic power, even when they aren't read, even when no one opens their pages. Books are inhabited by terrible demons, wicked sorcerers.

They disturb the peace of her home, a standing menace.

Helped by the barber, the curé performs an auto-da-fé upon the books of Don Quixote. Strangely, however, he saves a few books from the fire (among them *Amadis of Gaul*) and condemns them merely to be buried in a dry well. He's clearly less rigorous than the niece, who would not spare a single book. The curé only gets rid of those he finds mediocre as works of literature. His censorship is that of a critic, a lover of books. In other words, he's read all the chivalric and pastoral romances, exactly like Don Quixote, and isn't immune to the evil they spread. Mimetic contagion doesn't spare the other characters either, beginning with the innkeeper, who, familiar with the codes of chivalry, plays the role of castellan to perfection and provides Quixote with his knightly arms. The Canon of Toledo censures novels, but writes one himself. The wealthy and beautiful Marcella "roams from country to country in a shepherdess' costume"; the bachelor Samson Carrasco disguises himself as The Knight of the Mirror and the Knight of the White Moon; Sancho Panza takes possession of "his island" and assumes the responsibilities of government. All those around Don Quixote do nothing but chase after him, enter into his playacting, and pretend to be someone they're not— so much so that the reader sometimes asks himself whether they aren't madder than the Knight of the Mournful Countenance. All of them, to differing degrees, are inclined to quixotism. All of them, except the niece ...

•

Cut off from his comic books, Abdallah was miserable. But he had acquired the habit of reading and when he opened *Quest for Fire* he discovered, to his astonishment, that he was capable of following the novel's twists and turns. He read *Treasure Island, The Adventures of Arthur Gordon Pym, The Gold Hunters, The Prairie, Moby Dick, The Mutineers of the Bounty.* By dint of reading novels of the sea, he learned to swim.

Because most were illustrated novels, he was tempted to stop reading and look at the pictures. Proceeding in this way, he would learn the characters' fates ahead of time and feel that he was cheating, that he had become a voyeur. He was also tempted, when the book had no pictures, to skip past pages or chapters to find out what happened to the heroes and reassure himself that they didn't die, that they escaped from their enemies—the ravenous wolves, the avalanche, shipwreck, thirst and hunger. In any case, the chapter titles often gave away the ending of an adventure. The last chapter of one book by Jules Verne is "Saved!"

He quickly understood that the novel is an ambiguous, even untrustworthy kind of book, and that in this sense it was fundamentally different from the comic strip, whose cheerful, high-spirited, and optimistic tone never deceived the reader, or very rarely so. One couldn't appreciate this difference while reading the novels of James Oliver Curwood, who loved his characters so much that he never let them suffer a tragedy of any sort. It would sometimes happen that they became lost during their travels across the Arctic, but sooner or later they would find their way again.

When they were wounded it was nothing more than a scratch, the bullet never hit bone. A good meal, a sound night of sleep, and there they would be, back on their feet and with their high spirits restored. Curwood watched over them like an affectionate father; he was always there, when all seemed lost, to rescue them and reassure the needlessly anxious reader. This wasn't the case with other novels, in which the possibility of some terrible turn of events wasn't out of the question. Pym sets out on a fearful adventure that ends, unhappily, in front of a wall of ice; captain Ahab and his crew meet an apocalyptic end. There are nearly as many horrors in *Treasure Island* as in *The Adventures of Arthur Gordon Pym*, but there's an enormous difference in tone between, for example, the episode in which Jim, hidden inside a barrel of apples, overhears Long John Silver readying the mutiny, and the scene in which Pym, hidden away in the bilge, is made to confront his maddened dog in the darkness. Jim's friends are saved; those of Pym die one after another. Poe behaves like a merciless God, indifferent to suffering. He treats his characters—whether good or evil—with evenhandedness, forbidding himself to intervene in their affairs. They are his creations and he could redirect their destiny, or change the course of events, but instead he remains impassive, untroubled, idle—as if powerless in the world he himself created.

Each time he skipped a passage Abdallah felt some invisible being was watching him and frowning at his disloyalty. Breaking the linear order and opting for this barbaric, anarchic method of reading, he proved himself unworthy of the trust placed in him by the author, or more exactly (since the idea of an author was rather hazy in his mind), by the book. He made amends, once his curiosity was satisfied, by retracing his steps and reading the pages he had thoughtlessly skipped. This compromise between a perverse desire and the constraint of sequence didn't really absolve him. The compromise was one-sided. The text hadn't authorized it. He was behaving like one of those djinns that rashly fly up to the heavens, trying to learn the future history of the world and mankind. But the future belongs to God; anyone who attempts to travel there, to meddle in its affairs, is guilty of sacrilege.

What a relief for the reader to learn this barbaric manner of reading is an acknowledged, even codified method! The palindrome is a group of words that can be read either from left to right or right to left while keeping the same sense. Hariri composed several long texts that have one sense when read from beginning to end and another when read from the end to the beginning. Theorists praise the fragment—the text with multiple points of entry, whose sense is sporadic and fractured—and advocate reading against the grain. They argue that to give oneself an idea of how a text was composed, one must examine the last episode first, then the next-to-last, and in this way go back in time (which is to say, in the text) to the beginning.

Hurry was the first to recommence hostilities. Whether this proceeded from policy, an idea that he might gain some advantage by making a sudden and unexpected assault, or was the fruit of irritation and his undying hatred of an Indian, it is impossible to say. His onset was furious, however, and at first it carried all before it. He seized the nearest Huron by the waist, raised him entirely from the platform, and hurled him into the water, as if he had been a child. In half a minute, two more were at his side, one of whom received a grave injury by the friend who had just preceded him.

At that very moment a large hand stretched out and snatched away the book. Coming to his senses, Abdallah realized that while he was reading this passage from Fenimore Cooper's *The Deerslayer*, his father had been sitting right next to him. He was caught red-handed. His father, it's true, didn't read French, but the passage was illustrated with an especially eloquent picture, and it was this incriminating image that Muhammed was now examining. Some violent action was imminent. Abdallah, whose report cards were still catastrophically bad, would once again be confronted with all his father's accumulated grievances against comic books, this time directed against novels. But nothing of the sort occurred. Muhammed gave the book back without a word.

For years, Abdallah was incapable of explaining this sudden indulgence. Apathy? Contempt? Disappointment? No, the reason was quite different: his father hadn't taken the book away to punish him, but simply to look at the picture. He was lured by the image of Hurry throwing an Indian into the water and needed to have the book between his hands to look at it more closely, to see it for himself.

Having succumbed to the charm of the image, he was utterly disarmed and unable to carry out his duties as iconoclast and censor.

Tomorrows That Sing

EVERYTHING WAS TURNED upside-down when that young woman, whom we supposed to be a kind of nurse (no doubt because she looked after our health), but who was in fact a kind of social worker or inspector, came to see us at summer camp. And yet, to tell the truth, nothing was turned upside down. It was no big deal, not really, just a small wobble. Our condition didn't change in any profound manner, and hardly at all.

But let's begin at the beginning. On the walls of our classroom were images showing scenes of rural idyll: work, planting, the harvest, picking grapes. There were sheep, cows, and fowl, along with a fox and a wolf straight from the fables of La Fontaine. There was also a little hut, in which each of us dreamed of taking refuge. In our textbooks, too, there were often forests, woodcutters, shepherds, granaries, and each text was accompanied by an illustration that represented, for us city kids, the world beyond the town, a forever unreachable elsewhere—unless we might reach it by going to summer camp. There, we were promised passage into the fantastical world of our picture books— the images would open up into three dimensions, welcoming us onto their stage.

And so we went. Camp fare, which was mostly pasta, mashed vegetables, and sardines in oil, we enjoyed for its novelty. But after two or three days we had to face the facts: there wasn't enough of it. We were dying of hunger. Was it the fresh air that made us so ravenous? Fond memories of home-cooked meals? The fact of finding oneself in a crowd of campers who, as soon as the meals arrived, all turned into wolves? Food was always the main topic of conversation and we were in unanimous agreement that we never ate our fill. We brought up the matter with our camp counselors, who listened to us attentively, without speaking. They didn't eat with us, but rather with the superintendent, at a side table. They must not have been good eaters, since they always left their plates scandalously half-full. As for the director, he ate at home with his wife, a fantastically beautiful creature, and his two incredibly well-dressed children (they didn't wear our uniform), who never mixed with us. We couldn't identify the meals prepared for them by the cook, so we couldn't really be envious of this food, but the bananas, the apples, and especially the slices of melon and watermelon—these drove us wild with jealousy in the midday heat. We were like cats and dogs, watching their master eat and desperately hoping that some morsel might fall to the ground.

We ate little but, by way of compensation, we sang a lot. We spent the best part of our days singing. We sang when we got out of bed, before and after breakfast. We sang while heading off to the forest and also coming back. We sang before and after lunch. We didn't sing during the siesta, which lasted until four o'clock. These hours we had to remain absolutely silent and sleep, or pretend to sleep (our counselor would leaf for a few minutes through a book of poems by Alfred de Musset, then fall into a deep slumber). But we sang after the siesta and again while heading off to the forest, where we played elaborate games (I don't remember any of them), interrupted, of course, with singing. We sang on the way back. There was yet more singing before dinner, a dozen songs in the evening, and finally we went to bed.

We were happy. The proof: we sang. One doesn't sing unless one is happy. Of course sad songs exist—nostalgic, heart-rending songs that bring tears to the eyes—but our songs were very cheerful, redolent of good fortune and well-being. We sang of the beauty and vitality of nature: flowers, trees, waterfalls, mountains, mountaintops. We sang of virtuousness in general and of individual virtues: work, solidarity, the team spirit that makes us strong, healthy bodies and healthy minds. We didn't forget the laborer in his field, nor the mason with his brick wall, nor the woodworker who, surrounded by his saws, also sang. Above all (I was about to forget), we sang of birds, for we ourselves were birds. Light, free, and unburdened, we communicated by singing, just like those winged creatures. What could be more marvelous than to give up prose and to express oneself entirely in verse? Our existence was blessed by the grace of poetry and music; our days were measured by songs, whose subjects varied with the time of day. In the morning we sang of the morning and at night we sang of the night. We did not sing of the night in the morning, nor of the morning at night—that would have been to turn the cosmic order inside out. We, however, lived in symbiosis with the cosmos, in a perfect harmony, accompanying its flow with a language that was its mirror image. Indeed, our language had such presence, was so imposing and real, that by comparison the cosmos seemed redundant. The day dawned and the night fell in order that we should sing them. If they could no longer be sung, they would cease to exist. Night and day would disappear forever. Our songs had a demiurgic force: they might do without creation, but creation was inconceivable without our singing.

In the evening, birds (which must have been sparrows) gathered in the foliage of the chestnut tree in the middle of the camp, where they sang all together. Were they paying their respects to the setting sun? Was this their way of praying, of expressing their joie de vivre? Or did they rather seek to ward off the terrors of night by a display of solidarity? There were at least a hundred birds in the foliage and they produced a deafening, stupefying concert. Each sought to sing the loudest, to make his voice ring out above the others. Woe to him who did not sing. In this mood of aggressive competition, he would be banished or pecked to pieces by his fellows; he would no longer find a mate, and he would die. A rigid hierarchy assigned each sparrow his place in the foliage. To keep it, he had to show the group that he played an active part in the vesperal concert.

We loved to sing. We sang as we breathed. Some members of the group showed an especially praiseworthy zealousness: they burst into song even when the counselor, perhaps meditating on a verse by de Musset, forgot to make us sing. They reminded him of his duty and soon we were all singing. These were the fanatics, singing until their last breath. Everywhere was summer camp to them. At official functions they would be the first to clap, obliging others to follow. They were so full of enthusiasm that they would clap even when there was no need. A simple smacking together of the hands and their joy would communicate itself to everyone.

There were others, one must admit, who didn't like to sing. They regretted having come to camp and each morning counted the days that were left. For these campers, the days crept forward slowly, painfully, full of songs. Tired of fighting, they had recourse to a bit of trickery, opening and closing their mouths without any sound. They cheated. This wasn't done without feelings of guilt, for they were out of sync and had no part in the general good cheer. The counselor watched them suspiciously, their eyes lacking the hard brilliance that characterizes the true singer. Found out, the counselor sidled up close to them or moved them squarely into the first row to preempt any further mischief.

So they agreed to compromise and sang in a middle register without putting forth too much effort. From time to time they raised their voices to show their good will, but only so that a moment later they might break the rules in silence.

These troublemakers have sealed their fate at summer camp. Back at school they will rediscover the subjects of these songs in their textbooks, or as themes for composition. But this will pose no problem as they are by now well trained. Thanks to the camp counselors they've learned—and there's no going back—the gap between thought and word, the irreparable tear between being and seeming. They've learned to show joy while being miserable, to sing while being hungry. They've learned the art of doing a thing while crossing one's fingers, the arts of dissimulation and deception. Asked to write a theme for composition, they will know what the instructor wants from them. Should one get up late, or early? They spot the trap right away. They write that one should rise at dawn in conformity with the natural order of things. They add that one should also go to bed early for in this way one will enjoy good health, work productively, etc. Do you prefer to read comic books or to do your homework? We prefer to do our homework, by God! Later, they will hold all assemblies and crowds in horror, will flee from souks, public events, and gallery openings. They are invariably courteous, discreet, and loyal to their friends, but detest soccer (except where the national team is concerned: then, out of weakness, they watch the match on television, but nothing in the world could force them to go to the stadium). One will not often see them at the mosque. Shy, and attached to their habits, they lead an intense spiritual life, but tend to pray at home, or in the privacy of their hearts. They won't join a political party or speak at gatherings. In short, they will be bad citizens. Until their dying day, these hypocrites will make a pretense of singing, opening and closing their mouths without uttering a word.

We were in the middle of singing, just before lunch, when the "nurse" arrived. She got out of the car and the director hurried to greet her. She was neither beautiful nor ugly. She spoke French, and whenever she switched to our tongue we had the impression of hearing an unknown sort of Arabic, new and surprising. But she certainly wasn't French, and despite her short hair she had the face of a fellow countrywoman. Full of energy, diligent, busy as a bee, she spoke to the counselors and then came to see us, going from table to table, tasting our food, and engaging us in long conversations. We marveled at her impeccable French, which was easy, crisp, and direct. She left us to see the director again. They spoke for some time, walking about all the while (for some mysterious reason the director shook his head and waved his hands in the air). Finally she got back in her car and disappeared, raising a cloud of dust. Aside from French women, we had never seen a female drive. That day, unlike all the others, we didn't sing after breakfast, and the siesta was shorter than usual.

Two or three days later, as we were about to begin our twelve evening songs, the director stood up in the shadows. He had a letter in his hand. He greeted us with the traditional "Katikatikati" (a word that belongs to no language, but which in our camp meant: silence, attention, alert). We responded with the no less traditional "AAA," a triple vowel that more or less signified: message received, we're on guard, our attitude is attentive and respectful. It was the first time he was addressing us and we supposed he had some weighty matter to communicate.

"My children," he said, surrounded by a heavy silence, "we form one large family here. I treat you exactly as I do my own two sons, who share along with you the joys of summer recess—a recess in which the useful is joined with the pleasurable, where the school and its educational mission are prolonged and reinforced. I spare no effort to make sure this time is beneficial to you, you the men of tomorrow, you upon whom weighs the great responsibility of building our country. Your counselors, who have been adequately trained, look after you with devotion and a feeling of obligation. As for you, my children, I can only congratulate myself for your upright and honorable conduct. But a family that sticks together, happy and harmonious, provokes jealousy. Wicked people, working in the shadows, seek to break it apart. Just so, that woman who arrived a few days ago—that unbeliever who drives herself around in a car— has gone to the capital to tell her superiors that you here are badly fed. This claim is a base calumny, a vile attack, and

a black defamation. Our response must be vigorous. Therefore your counselors will write a letter, in your name, to the
capital, revealing the dark designs of the unbeliever. May
God the All-Mighty and All-Knowing give her the punishment she deserves."

That night we sang, under the skillful conducting of the
director, two dozen songs. During the days that followed
we noticed no change in our diet. There was only a vague
uneasiness in the air.

The day of departure finally arrived. We rushed quickly
through our morning songs, simply to earn the right to
breakfast. Another song—the last, the best—already gal-
loped through our heads:

> *Let's go children, time to leave*
> *Everyone must go home*
> *Heads full of songs*
> *Hearts full of memories*
> *Let's go children, time to leave*
> *Let's go children, 'til next time*

We sang this in a mood of shared excitement, a fever-
ishness that gripped us as we packed our bags. The song-
fanatics, the future hand-clappers—they wept. As for the
hypocrites, they became birds at last, singing their heads
off with a pleasure and enthusiasm they had never before
exhibited. They took their revenge, beaming with happi-
ness. There was no more need for the counselor to lead the

singing. And anyway, where were the counselors? It didn't matter, they no longer existed, were nowhere to be seen. They'd become stray ghosts, pitiful shades. In the train that delivered us quickly to the capital we babbled with joy. We called out from one compartment to another, from one car to another, "Katikatikati! AAA!" The train was one rollicking song. *Let's go children, 'til next time …*

Next time? No way! Good-bye, a final and irrevocable good-bye. They would never recapture us.

Pleiades

NO LONGER ABLE to visit her, Layla's madman paced in front of her home, covering it in kisses. This is how he proclaimed his love to the world while caressing, metonymically, his beloved. Abdallah was less courageous and made do, once a day, with walking past the street where Pleiades lived (Thurayya, the Arabic name, was taboo, unpronounceable for him). He glanced quickly up the street and then hurried on his way, anxious that his passion, of which he was all but unconscious, might explode into the open and cover him in shame. Hidden behind a wall, he watched Pleiades as she left for school, following her with his eyes until she disappeared. At times, by accident of his peregrinations through the streets (where he sought her constantly), they would meet face to face. Without pausing, she would smile at him sweetly. She was four years older than he.

What surprised him, at each encounter, was the quickened and excessive beating of his heart. He talked about this with Fat Ali, an infallible exegete, who told him: "It's because you love her!" This was a revelation for Abdallah: he was in love and didn't know it. Fat Ali assigned a definite meaning to that beating heart, to the excitement caused by that face's sudden apparition. He gave birth to love by naming it. A fleeting, fugitive sensation became explicit— one word and the veil covering this unacknowledged truth was swept aside. All this came to Abdallah as a relief (he finally understood what was happening to him) and, at the same time, as a kind of betrayal: what he felt toward Pleiades wasn't new, wasn't original, was nothing but an imitation of similar experiences already described in books. Literature waited for Abdallah at every turn—he consulted it to find out how he should feel, think, and act, and henceforth found himself there as in a mirror.

But what sort of love should he dedicate himself to? The heroic love of knightly romances? The idyllic, sisterly love of Daphnis and Chloe, Paul and Virginia? The worldly love of novels by Balzac and Maupassant? The tragic love of Romeo and Juliet, Werther and Charlotte? The nostalgic, coy love ("Yes, I want to love you, but just a little bit") of Apollinaire? Abdallah couldn't range his love under any of these categories. The only kind he knew was the love of those who didn't dare admit their love—who, out of prudence or because they believed their love was not reciprocated, never seized the occasion to declare themselves. These lovers go to great lengths to meet but once in each other's presence they retreat, or lose their nerve. In the end, however, some happy coincidence opens their eyes to the truth. Then their joy is equaled only by that of the reader (or audience), who has known of their secret passion from the outset, who has willed them into each other's arms, hands thrown up to the sky at their disobedience.

Alas, Pleiades did not love Abdallah in secret but was openly enamored of Benmarouf, a hipster with pegged pants and slicked back hair à la Clark Gable, who threw parties and invited girls who were pretty, modern, and aggressive. Along with their boyfriends they formed a tight clique, jealous of its privileges and completely inaccessible to outsiders. Stationed behind a streetlamp, Abdallah would watch and wait all afternoon for Pleiades to arrive, enthralled by the wild music of Elvis Presley, which spread menacingly from Benmarouf's home out into the neighboring streets.

In the evening, having accompanied Pleiades home (albeit from a distance), he returned, downcast, to his own house and composed poems about the starry sky. Fat Ali, who was little inclined to fantasy (but who nevertheless claimed, based on a reputable source, that it was the custom among Christians for a married women to be deflowered on her wedding day not by her husband but by the parish priest) refused to give his opinion of Abdallah's verses. "Anyway," he would say, "poetry is pointless." This did not prevent Fat Ali from citing at every opportunity (just to get Abdallah's goat) these starry verses of Omar ibn Abi Rabi'a:

You who would marry the Pleiades to the constellation of Canopus,
How—may God make your life a long one—how will they meet?

And yet Abdallah did not stop arranging his alexandrines and octosyllabics, convinced that when he became a great poet (which wouldn't be long, since Rimbaud was one at sixteen), Pleiades, drawn by the widespread admiration of which he was the object, would soften her heart, turn toward him, and fall in love. But Fat Ali, who didn't call anyone 'Canopus except Abdallah, finally put him out of his misery by recounting this terrible scene: in the presence of her female friends, those glamorous co-conspirators, Pleiades removed a photo of Benmarouf from her bra and ate it.

"Yeah," Ali went on, "she chewed it up and then she swallowed it."

Then, for no apparent reason, he recited a verse from the *sura* of Yousef: "The women of the city told each other of what had happened saying, 'The wife of the Lord of Egypt wished to take pleasure with his slave, who had made her mad with passion. She is truly lost.'" He crowed with pleasure, unaware, or hardly at all, of the mischief he sowed with this story.

Abdallah tried to forget Pleiades, in vain. He experienced his love as a failing, a regression, a piece of cowardice. Nor did his reading provide any models to reassure or encourage him by showing him that his case wasn't unique. He had just turned thirteen and, knowing neither how to free himself nor how to wait, believed he would always be unlucky in love. A few years later Pleiades' feelings underwent an unexpected change and one evening, under a tree, she kissed him. Surprise, exaltation. Her lips were humid and melting, like ripe fruit; her mouth was open, juicy, soft. The verse of Mallarmé, "It was the blessed day of your first kiss," sprung inevitably to his lips, along with the bitter-sweet aftertaste of an old photograph.

Cinédays

EVERY FRIDAY I WENT to the cinema, anxious and trembling with desire, like a lover who goes to meet his beloved, unsure whether she'll honor their date. Though I showed up two hours early and was first in line in front of the ticket window, I invariably found myself at the back of the line when the tickets came on sale, and oftentimes that awful phrase, "Sold Out," cast me back into daylight when all I wanted was to be swallowed in shadows. When I did manage to get a ticket another agony began: my confrontation with the attendant, a stodgy Spanish woman who insisted on a tip. It was all I could do to obtain the seventy centimes I needed to pay for my seat, a sum wrested from my mother after a fight worthy of the Atrides. The attendant insulted me, but despite my fears she didn't chase me off. So I took my seat, terrified by the mob of hilarious faces surrounding me, a frightened Little Tom Thumb among the ogres—big ruffians who guzzled bottles of lemonade and ate popcorn and mille-feuilles.

At last the first film began, stripped of its credit sequence—which was usually long, with too many names, and anyway no one in the audience could read English. I didn't understand much from the images marching aimlessly in front of my eyes, but after watching many westerns ("cowboy films," as they were called), I did acquire a certain vocabulary, later enriched by my reading of comic books: the tomahawk, the mustang, the fort, the Winchester, the squaw, the colt, the teepee (also known as the wigwam), the buffalo, and, of course, the sheriff. In short, the keywords of a genre studded with famous names: Jeff Chandler, Sitting Bull, Alan Ladd, Manitou, Fort Apache, Cochise, Geronimo. I didn't go to watch any particular film. Unable to follow the plot, I was only interested in the formulaic scenes, which are interchangeable and form a world unto themselves: the duel, the mount-up, the Indian attack on the fort, the brawl in the saloon, and—one mustn't forget—the kiss.

Certain set-ups left no doubt as to how things would end. When two women covet a single hero the problem is almost always solved in the same fashion. As if by chance, one is a brunette and the other a blond: two skin types, two opposing temperaments. The brunette is often a bargirl, a saloonkeeper, friend to the outlaw chief (recognizable by his black outfit, watch chain, cigars, and the honeyed smile that is given the lie by his cruel stare). Self-assured, a drinker, a smoker, aggressive, and spoiling for a fight, the brunette quickly overwhelms the hero with her arrogance and scorn. The blond is younger, naive, pure, awkward, and therefore sympathetic; she arouses the desire to protect and finally to marry her. But the brunette isn't truly bad. Her show of disdain spurs the hero to prove what he's made of, demonstrate his true mettle, stand up for himself. Eventually she begins to admire him. Her glances, full of meaning, reveal that she's secretly in love. But the brunette is compromised by the company she keeps. Caught in a terrible bind, she becomes more and more pitiable, for now it is the hero who heaps his scorn on her. So she must be sacrificed, made to disappear for good. She has just enough time to save the hero from certain death before meeting her own fate at the hands of her former protector. In this way she redeems her tainted past. As she breathes her last, the hero leans over her and is assailed with the sense of a debt he can never pay back. A feeling of bitterness wells up, just like the one that follows a massacre of redskins.

This ending did not please the audience at all. Their well-developed sense of justice revolted against the fate meted out unfairly to the brunette. She saved the hero's life and her only reward is death? Intolerable! And all this to benefit the blond, who proved, from one end of the film to the other, that she was a complete scatterbrain! Whistles of protest broke out. We couldn't change the story (whatever we had understood of it) but we weren't going to witness this travesty without an vigorous response.

At such moments we blamed the projectionist, a luminary whom we never saw. One might cross paths with him in the lobby but no one could pick him out of a crowd.

We only knew that he kept to a little box above the ticket booth. We heard the scratching of his machine in the darkness and, twisting around, one could see the stream of light he let escape from a small hole in the wall. As if by magic, he caused a whole world to spring to life on the screen. Before his intervention there was nothing, and then suddenly, simply by virtue of this invisible being's decision, something happened. Let it be! Out of nothing a universe was born, fully constituted, perfect. The demiurge was all the more impressive in that he also had the power to destroy what he had made. Let it not be! The obedient earth and sky began to shiver and then disappeared entirely, returning to the nothing from whence they had so miraculously been brought forth.

While the projectionist rethreaded his defective film, the anxious spectators shook themselves free from the debris of this uncreated world. They rose up from their graves like resurrected dead on the Day of Judgment. And here was the last trumpet, the dead coming back to life with a symphony of whistles. Then the film resumed and the world reappeared, just as it was at the moment it had been interrupted. The characters started up again, not realizing they had been engulfed in non-being. They continued chatting, moving about as if nothing had happened, as if they had not just escaped a terrible catastrophe, as if they had not just been tossed into a bottomless chasm.

In addition to cuts caused by the bad quality of the film there were others due purely to the will of the projection-

ist. Having gorged on images, and tired now of seeing the
same scenes over and over, he must have had only one wish:
to leave, to escape the theater's unwholesome airs. So he
cut by a third the two films he projected for each showing, skipping over the scenes he didn't like or that seemed
to him superfluous, purely decorative. In this way, in absolute good faith, he protected the audience from boredom.
His censorship was meant to be affirmative and enhanc-
ing. It made the film characters leap about in an extraordinary fashion—leaps that carried them outside of time and
place. A sheriff might be comfortably seated in his office,
legs up on a table, the end of a cigar between his lips and
a bottle of whiskey within easy reach. A fraction of a second later he finds himself in the middle of a desert, fighting an Indian who lifts his tomahawk to deliver the fatal
blow. The sheriff doesn't know how he's been cast into this
nightmare, doesn't know that he has passed from one di-
mension to another, and that part of his life, gone without
a trace, has been stolen behind his back.

As for the audience, they know the projectionist has
double-crossed them. But, taken by surprise and thrown
directly into the fight sequence, they don't respond, saving
their vengeance for later. The wild-eyed sheriff manages to
gather himself at the last moment. Dodging the blow that
would have split his skull, he shoots the Indian and then
reins up, looking all around, evidently wondering where he
is, how he got there, and what could possibly have transpired since the moment he was comfortably seated in his

office. He'll never find out. The projectionist is a thief of time, a raider of memory.

But woe to the projectionist who skipped a fight, or a kiss—something he would never do, in any case, for fear of the public but also because he too savored these choice morsels. We counted kisses, comparing them to one another in the same way that we kept track of those bandits whom the hero took down with his fists and those he took out with his revolver. Kisses provoked a more violent reaction than the one caused by cuts. Protestations, insults, threats, obscenities—nothing was spared the hero, who had been up to this point admired and encouraged. As soon as he put his lips on the heroine's he was utterly despised. That he should triumph over miscreants was something everyone wished for, but for him to embrace the frail and tearful heroine—this was judged an insult and a betrayal. Why him and not us? The indignant spectators could barely restrain themselves from getting up to teach him a lesson and tear the heroine from his lusty embrace. Each of us felt he'd been robbed, cheated of what was rightfully his. Our indignation reached its peak when the heroine gave in without resistance—when, taking the hero in her arms, she showered him with ardent kisses. As soon as she closed her eyes in abandonment, we rose up and called her every name in the book, pouring the most abject insults on her head.

In other words, the public was ambivalent. So long as the hero courted the heroine and treated her with devotion, we noisily and vigorously championed him. But as soon as he touched her, as soon as he kissed her—a promise made real—everything was ruined. The hero was like some special envoy whose mission was to kiss the heroine, but who is quickly rejected by the public. Each of us had the unpleasant impression of embracing a ghost, even as the hero wrapped his arms around a young and delectable woman. In the tumult surrounding this kiss-by-mandate, no one cared to remember that hero and heroine were nothing but shadows projected on a screen.

There were, however, some films without kisses. Consider the following scene: the heroine, wearing a kerchief on her head, holds herself upright, not far from the saloon. She is pale and tired (the kerchief, knotted beneath her chin, accentuates this impression). It seems to be the final scene. The audience doesn't know the reason for the young woman's weariness, only that there was a terrible misunderstanding at some point in the past and that she's been angry with the hero (there's a glimmer of enmity in her clear blue eyes). But some time has passed. Several satisfactory battles have transpired, a night around the campfire (with beans and coffee doled out to unshaven and surly cowboys), a spectacular chase, a buffalo stampede that nearly charged off the screen, and many, many deaths. Now everything is back to normal. It is evening, a lazy tune escapes from the saloon. The young woman appears to have been left alone in a patch of shadow (she may have done something wrong). The hero comes slowly toward her. The audience holds its breath. A reconciliation seems imminent, yet one can't be sure, given their violent disagreement in the past. The hero finally comes to a halt in front of his old rival. A long kiss? No, something worse—he begins untying the heroine's kerchief. "Put your paws down!" a spectator cries from the orchestra. "Let him do it!" responds another from the balcony (as if the action depended on their good will). The kerchief untied, a strand of blond hair suddenly emerges, lit with sudden brilliance. The heroine looks at the hero tenderly. She smiles at him. Suddenly, "The End" writes itself on the screen. Lights.

The longed-for (and greatly feared) kiss did not come to pass. After the first moment of surprise, and after looking at one another with a sense of having been duped, the spectators guess that the projectionist has double-crossed them again. But those who can read say he has nothing to do with it. The spectators don't then blame the director or producer (ideas totally unfamiliar to them) but rather the cinema, where they happen to find themselves. They throw bottles at the curtain and tear up the seats; a fight breaks out between two opposing groups and soon the theater looks like a saloon in the middle of a brawl.

The audience's expectations were disappointed. But this frustration was probably anticipated and even planned for by the director. Certainly it wasn't prudery that made him withhold the kiss. On the contrary, the originality of this ending, the unknotted kerchief, is that it authorizes all sorts of hypotheses, all sorts of daydreams, even the most outrageous and indecent. The spectators must have sensed it, but didn't want to acknowledge that the hero was undressing the young woman (in the jargon of rhetoric this is called a synecdoche, the part for the whole). And perhaps, for some of them, the dream of possessing a woman would henceforth appear under the guise of an unknotted headscarf, a discreet gesture that frees a lock of hair, a golden fleece heretofore hidden.

The projectionist only cut scenes with dialogue—of which he understood not a word—and the spectators, in their heart of hearts, thanked him for it. Their whistling, far from being angry, was purely formal, a way of registering the cut and signaling that they weren't fooled. Indeed, when he forgot to edit a scene of dialogue, boring by definition, low whistles reminded him of the unspoken agreement, scolding him and calling him to attention. It was his fault if the spectators were bored. They wanted action, exploits. Enough talking, enough repartee, explanations, lessons (for example, that never-ending lesson given by a mustachioed officer to his subordinates while pointing with his little stick to a map hanging on the wall). That was all dead time, filler, hokum. Because they couldn't understand the links between the various episodes of the film, the audience was never fully absorbed by it and remained on high alert, looking out in particular for one of the projectionist's tricks. Keeping their distance, albeit against their will, the spectators never gave in to the illusion (except of course when there was a fight or a kiss) and in their own manner assumed control of how the film played out. They talked to the screen, exchanged commentaries, threw spit-balls, peanut shells, oranges. For them, going to the cinema was to perform a ritual, to share a common sentiment, to feel in concert and confirm their agnatic solidarity. Some-times they whistled for no reason, simply for the pleasure of whistling together, in a rapture of communication. In this way, alongside the spectacle that unfurled up on the screen, there was another down below—mocking, polyvocal, dis-cordant, clamorous.

The public of the Star (that was the name of my movie house) never ventured into the cinemas of the modern city. In the first place, tickets were more expensive; also, they only showed one film (what a racket!); finally, it was foreign territory, a place inhabited mostly by the French, who were all elegant, refined, aloof, cold, and, in short, beyond hope. In their presence one couldn't permit oneself the slightest impropriety, the softest whistle (and what was the use, any-way, since there were no cuts to protest?). One had to hold one's tongue and suppress one's feelings to the point of be-coming ill. And to see what? Films with incomprehensible titles: *Port of Shadows, Golden Helmet, Rififi, Gate of Lilacs, Wages of Fear.* True, some showed half-naked women with magnificent, bouncy breasts. And yet, before reaching that point, what dialogues, what boredom! Never a good fight, never the shadow of an Indian, just talking—lots of talking.

One day, to everyone's surprise, a French couple hap-pened into the Star. We felt vaguely honored by their presence and appreciated their discretion, for they had purchased the least expensive seats, down in the orchestra. Everything went well at first. The two guests were open-minded enough to tolerate our chatter during the film, and our smoking, even though it was technically forbidden (the wife, however, waved the smoke away from her face impatiently). But things took a turn for the worse at the first cut. The French were as indignant as the natives, the only difference being that they, the French, were serious. They were upset with the projectionist and made this clear by their murmurs and small gestures of irritation. Unfortunately the whistling continued, which prevented them from concentrating on the dialogue. The husband began to get agitated. He was still inclined to forgive, so long as the projectionist didn't repeat his crime and their neighbors stopped making such a ruckus. Not only were there more cuts, however, but just as things seemed to be back under control—the audience calm, the characters on screen conversing—just at that moment the whistling burst forth again, as sudden as it was irrational. Turning to his wife, the brave Gaul said: "I understand that they whistle when there's a cut, but why whistle when there isn't one?" In the end, however, he understood that there was a profound complicity between projectionist and public, that they were deliberately egging each other on, that they were engaged in some kind of game and were having a good time. And so, with the terrible sensation of having lost his way amongst fools, he grabbed his wife and exited the theater.

I have to admit that I didn't know how to whistle and

that I always felt this to be a weakness, a sign of inferiority, and a badge of exclusion. Even today it isn't without a certain envy that I see children place two fingers between their lips and whistle so easily and so happily.

Not long ago I went to see an Abel Gance film at the Trocadero Cinema in Paris. The picture wasn't very good and at one point the film stopped running. The lights came back on and everybody looked at each other, somewhat shyly and shamefacedly, as though waking from a nap that had caught them unawares. While dozing off we all had the same dream, exactly the same. Each had discovered an inner voyeur and was now surprised by the presence of others who had all watched, through the keyhole, an identical scene. The theater breathed a small sigh of collective guilt (a feeling that arises at the end of all screenings when one gets up to leave, but which is stronger when the film is interrupted and no one can do anything except avoid looking at one another). Irritated and indulgent, standoffish and complicit, the spectators—a group of twenty at most— wanted to go back to sleep and rejoin the sweet dream that was now going up in smoke. In the cave whose lights had just come on they were freed of their chains, yet they wanted nothing more than to put the chains back on, to dive back into the darkness, lose consciousness of themselves and let their gazes glide over those fleeting, illusory, and deceitful images.

Suddenly there were two or three whistles, brief and timid. I was shocked. So even in Paris—in a cinema whose audience was, at least in principle, well schooled—there were people who whistled! Not ten seconds had gone by before a small man in shirtsleeves, half bald and with a nasty, determined air, confronted the audience: "No, this is too much," he shouted. "Do I look like I'm joking? Where do you think you are? This isn't a circus!" It was the projectionist. He singled me out with his glance, suspecting that I was behind the whistling. After this reprimand he walked out, furious, dignified. Of course no one answered back. I imagined him confronting the old habitués of the Star. They would have responded with shouts and vociferations, they would have shoved that reprimand back down his throat. A well-aimed orange would have landed smack on the bald part of his head.

For the first time, I had seen a projectionist. He was an ordinary man with ordinary passions, a technician who toiled over a commonplace machine, battling against a tide of tangled film wheels and anxiously insisting on the prestige of his position. He was a deposed and fallen god, a shrunken gnome. He had nothing in common with that transcendent being of long ago who liked to dialogue with the public by manipulating images—fantastical, playful, clownish, often challenged, but never in his capacity as Unmoved Mover and First Cause.

A Season in the Hammam

MANY MEN SPEAK of the hammam of their early childhood as a lost paradise. They would accompany their moth-
ers to that warm and humid place, brimming with magical,
female bodies. And then one day they had to stop accompanying their mother and resign themselves to going along
with the father. They had to leave the world of women to
enter the world of men and suffer, at around the age of five,
a second severance. So the maternal hammam is recalled
with nostalgia, as a paradise of infantile amours.

Personally, I've kept no memory of my first years at the
hammam. No memory, in any case, of young and vigorous
female bodies. The only image I retain of it (a memory? a
phantasm?) is of three ladies of a certain age, flabbily naked.
They stand at the entrance to the first chamber and are most
probably gossiping, for they form a circle looking at one another. One of them dangles a wooden bucket from her hand,
a bucket without a bottom. They'll never move from those

places, fixed for eternity in these same postures.

But let's leave these women, these Danaides with leaky buckets, to one side of our topic, to one side of our trip, and let's enter the hammam. Our steps lead us slowly but surely toward the overheated third chamber, where we'll find a basin full of boiling water. On the way we can see, amidst the humid chiaroscuro, silhouettes that stand or sit or lounge on their sides. We'll dip out some water from the streaming fountain, scrub ourselves briskly, then walk back out into the daylight, clean and comfortable in our bodies. All true enough, but we should also remark that in the meantime we've lived through the crucial moments of human existence as they have been imagined by religion: life and death, submission and revolt, merits and demerits, grace and punishment, hope and despair, the mundane and the transcendent, the appeal to God and the answer—never unambiguous—that falls from the sky.

It isn't only in the mosque where the believer lives and practices his faith; it isn't only by reading the Quran than he strengthens his ties with the sacred; the hammam is also a place of spiritual effervescence, where the believer experiences, in mind and body, an entire history, one in which his own destiny is writ large as the destiny of humankind in general. In the space of one hour, time contracts and condenses; the story of man's relations with this world, and with God, comes into a tight focus. This juxtaposition of hammam and mosque isn't altogether arbitrary: the hammam ensures the ritual purity of the body, a necessary preliminary to prayer. Nor is this all—the architecture of the hammam is centered around the basin of hot water, the structure's living heart, its pole of attraction, a magnetic center nothing escapes. One's itinerary through the hammam is predetermined, leading straight to the basin, which shouldn't fail to remind us of the mosque, where only one direction is possible—the direction of the mihrab, that niche cut into the wall and oriented toward Mecca.

But in contrast to the mosque, the hammam is also a site of risk, of the spectacular fall, for at any moment you might slip on the soapy tiles. You might also faint in the unbearable heat. And then—a vision of horror—you risk falling into the boiling basin every time you lean over to ladle out some water, a risk of being thrown into the depths of hell. Whoever crouches to plunge his bucket into the basin must resist the call of the abyss, the temptation of suicide, and, depending on the outcome of this roll of the dice, he'll know whether he's to be joined with the just and crowned with favors, or with the condemned who suffer divine wrath. For the hammam is a theater where a great day is being rehearsed: the Day of Judgment. All these bodies, slowly circulating as in a dream, or meeting silently in front of the basin—so many indistinct, interchangeable, naked bodies! The dimness doesn't allow their contours to stand out, and in any case they bear no sign that would indicate origin, social class, wealth or poverty, power or weakness. By imposing absolute uniformity, the hammam also imposes absolute equality, a foreshadowing of the Great

Day, when no one shall flatter themselves with any title, distinction, or privilege whatsoever.

Equality before God, equality before death. To go to the hammam is to die a little, to rehearse one's own passing. And when I say death I'm thinking not only of that utter exhaustion which invades the body and bends it toward the earth, that shortness of breath which quickly drives you from the hot chamber into one of the two others, with less inclement temperatures. When I say death I'm thinking also, and above all, of a precise experience: that of being with the masseur. This is a muscled character with tremendous energy—a djinn of the hammam, if you will—who seems to know no living, spoken language. While massaging you he lets out whistles with the tip of his tongue set against the teeth, sounds whose significance is yet to be discovered in the heart of I-know-not-what primitive or bestial darkness. You're completely at the mercy of this powerful personage. You depend on him, and submit to total inertia under his hands. You are dead, a corpse receiving its mortuary toilette. You and the dead have a number of things in common—nudity, inertia, proximity to the earth, and also the water, which purifies you and prepares you for your meeting with God. The masseur is a middleman, a washer of corpses, who does not knead your body with any hygienic or therapeutic goal. His role is more momentous, for he carries you across a frontier that separates the here-and-now from the beyond.

The hammam is a descent into the other world. One

does not rise into a hammam, one goes down into it (it's difficult to conceive of a hammam perched on high). As soon as you push open the door to enter the first chamber you must go down a step, at least one step. The hammam is located in the depths of the earth; as an underworld, it is necessarily a dark place, starless and sunless, far from the day and the night, outside all calendars and chronologies. The sun has no access to this world of the dead, this sojourn of shapeless shadows, which reflects only imperfectly the forms of the world above, the world bathed by the sun. The hammam is a dark glass on whose surface vague silhouettes and uncertain apparitions project themselves. You become the shadow of yourself as soon as you go down into its catacomb, a pit filled with thick and suffocating steam.

What are all these shades doing in this hellish place? They're waiting. They wait for the divine manifestation, the sign of epiphany, the oft-doubted announcement of deliverance. You know, of course, that the most precious substance in the hammam is water, hot water, which sometimes gushes forth but is very often scarce, parsimonious, and so gives rise to the most dramatic and terrible of scenes. Having scraped the bottom of the basin, the bathers, covered in sweat and holding empty buckets, crouch and wait for the providential waters to run once more. The great test begins, which is at first a test of language: one must communicate with the giver of water, that invisible being situated on the other side of the wall, the other side of the rock. His intentions are unfathomable yet everything depends on his good will. He might provide the water willingly, just as he might hold it back. Master of water and fire, his behavior is, to all appearances, utterly arbitrary.

It is with him, then, that one must communicate. But does he understand? Does he care about these weary shades in distress? Perhaps he's asleep, or perhaps he's not where one thinks he is; perhaps he's gone away, abandoning the bathers who depend upon him absolutely, like prisoners behind this wall of wailing. Despair sets in, and increases with each passing moment. One of the shadows, seized by a sudden rage, will sometimes grab a bucket and strike it against the wall of the basin, thereby mimicking an ancient gesture, that of Moses striking the rock with his staff, making water surge from the hard, deaf rock …

This one-way dialogue with the invisible being continues unabated, becoming more and more violent. The appeal of the bathers, hammered out repeatedly against the rock, is joined to the voice, to the word: "Let the water free!" they cry at the invisible being. But he doesn't respond. He doesn't respond to their speech with speech, nor to their blows with blows. He responds only with silence, a response so ambiguous that no one even knows if the message has been received. Confronted with this silence, with this wait that threatens to last forever, they take up the demand once more, crying out louder and louder. The tone of their appeal (and of their hammerings on the rock) changes, passing from beseechment and supplication to protestation and indignation, and even to threats and insults.

As the invisible being's silence becomes more and more intolerable, the bathers come together and decide to do something. One obviously can't continue roasting in one's skin and not try to escape such a hellish situation. But to extract a response from the master of water and fire, one must first make sure that he really has received the message. The last resort will be the hammam's watchman, a character I have so far neglected to mention, and who must be summoned immediately.

Seated peaceably next to the door, he watches those who come in and out. He is responsible for guarding the bathers' clothes, and, in his capacity as doorkeeper, mediates between the world outside and the world inside, the world of sun and the world of night, the world of solid bodies and the world of quavering ghosts, the world of clothing and the world of nudity, the world of the living and the world of the dead. It is to him the bathers will have recourse; he will be the messenger, the intermediary. He has a direct link to the invisible being and can go to him and talk face-to-face, whereas the shades are cut off from him by a sheer wall. The watchman's intercession produces a favorable response from the master of water and fire, and finally saves the community of shades.

The intercession doesn't always have an immediate effect. The invisible being, it would seem, likes to remain unpredictable, likes to underline the exceptional nature of his gift. The wait lengthens. The bathers turn their rage against the watchman, blaming him for the hardships they suffer, scapegoating him. And then, abruptly, the miracle occurs: a thin trickle of water begins to flow. The rock has at last softened, releasing liquid! The shades rejoice.

But they must still wait a while longer before serving themselves. They must wait for the basin to fill to the top, must organize the distribution of water and not succumb to indiscipline, must keep the welfare of the group foremost in mind. Any attempt to fill the buckets up at once, individually, can lead to nothing but confusion and chaos; everyone would try to serve himself first, fights would break out, and ultimately no one would get any water. This is not how things are done. From the mass of bathers one person quickly stations himself next to the basin, to defend it from any selfish designs. This is usually a solid sort of person, one whom no one has assigned the task of guarding the water, but who puts himself forward and graciously offers his services. He wields a tremendous power that is never contested, for his authority springs from the fact that he is the last to be served. This basin-dipper and water distributor shows an admirable fair-mindedness, providing an object lesson in abnegation and altruism. When the basin is full he shares out the water equally, never filling the buckets more than halfway the first time around. Finally each bather repairs to his corner, having strengthened his belief in community and experienced the pleasures of teamwork. The water continues to run and since everyone has already been served, the basin overflows. After impoverishment there is abundance, excess. But no one thinks of asking the invisible being to plug up this affluence.

Leaving the hammam, the bather climbs up from this chthonic realm toward the world of sunlight. He experiences resurrection after death. He's changed both clothes and skin, traded his old self for a new one. Near the hammam he may run into the fuel seller, using a stick to guide his donkey, laden with firewood and trailing in its wake a pleasant odor—the warm, sweet smell of wood. Always accompanied by his donkey, the fuel seller is one of the few who enjoy direct, personal contact with the invisible being. Deep in his cave, this being uses firewood and kindling to fuse water and fire, feeding the hot, incandescent magma that bubbles in the earth's intestines like an underground sun, a mirrored sun, whose rays rise up from below.

Nowadays, the donkey has disappeared. You'll no longer find one in the vicinity of the hammam. He's been replaced by a little truck. A minor, cosmetic, inessential alteration? When one element is disturbed the slippage spreads to others and finally the whole structure collapses. The donkey is replaced by the truck, the wood by coal, and so the pleasant odor of firewood and kindling is gone—also the link, however far-off and indirect, with the trees and forest. Nor are the hammam's buckets made of wood any more. At first the wood was replaced by I know not what kind of cold metal, hard and cutting, and then by some black plastic, dull and mournful.

More serious than the wood's disappearance is that of the basin, and its replacement by faucets, one in each of the three chambers. This means the heart of the hammam has stopped beating, a rupture whose immediate effect is panicked disorientation. For a hammam without a basin (or whose basin has ceased to work) is like a mosque without a mihrab: all directions are now possible and equally valid. There is no longer a magnetic pull leading ineluctably toward the fire; there is no longer that necessary itinerary leading from one chamber to another, ending in flames. All three chambers now have nearly the same temperature and so the three-part division of the hammam has no more reason to exist, the initiatory journey has lost its meaning.

Suddenly, the sacred character of the hammam is gone. If one need only turn a faucet to obtain hot water, what need to talk with the invisible being? And what of all this dialogue entails, of tribulation, risk, despair? The hammam is no longer a hammam: it's a public bath, a place of hygiene, nothing more. Things are no longer what they were. A great fragment of our childhood crumbles away.

The Magic Lamp

THE HERO OF A COMIC BOOK never dies. He undergoes many trials, of course: his enemies overpower him, take him as a prisoner, strap him to a torturer's chair. He may be badly wounded and even left for dead. His friends lament their loss, weeping over his body—but suddenly he opens his eyes, or heaves a weak sigh. He must have been pretending to be dead, or perhaps merely lost consciousness, or was only lightly wounded. A few days of rest and he's back on his feet, ready for new adventures.

A comic book hero doesn't die, cannot die, because he wasn't born. He has no parents and never did. Yet he is neither a bastard child nor a foundling. In fact, he escapes all genealogical classifications, all chains of transmission. Because he has no parents, he cannot become a father—he certainly can't give what he never received. Without a past or future, he simply is, and in this sense resembles God, "Neither begetting nor begotten, And none can be His peer."

When a character dies in a novel, they don't come back. A child who graduates from the comic book to Fenimore Cooper accomplishes a complicated feat of intellect. He becomes aware, for the first time, of the inevitable and irreparable nature of death. Uncas, last of the Mohicans, and the beautiful Cora, are killed in cowardly fashion by the sinister Magua, and there's no hope they'll return to life. In other words—and this is bitter knowledge—death doesn't spare the good. The world is not as it should be, as one had believed it was. It is only a small consolation when, during the funeral rites, the Indian women address themselves to Cora, who is no more, and promise her the green prairies of Manitou, where there is game in abundance. There she'll celebrate her nuptials with Uncas, will never lack for anything, and be forever happy. In their funerary dirge, the practical-minded Indians recommend that the dead woman "be attentive to the wants of her companion, and never to forget the distinction which the Manitou had so wisely established between them." But what's more affecting is when they ask her not to succumb to futile regrets for her loved ones and for the places where she once lived. What does this mean, except that nothing can console Cora for the loss she has suffered? The prairies of Manitou, however splendid, cannot distract her from the still fresh memory of her former life. Yet the Indians suggest that she must forget, must have nothing more to do with the past.

The dead person's first duty is to sever all ties with earthly life and give up his personhood. This he must do for the sake of those still living, as well as for himself. Only anonymity will grant him peace and reconcile him to his new existence. There are, however, some dead who refuse to drink the water of the Lethe. They suffer unheard-of torments. They wander ceaselessly through the places they once knew, and which are still familiar, but where no one now pays them any attention. They can't communicate with those dear ones for whom sadness is still a kind of comfort and painful consolation. At night they force their way into these dear ones' dreams, just long enough for a short conversation—no trace of which remains by morning. Sometimes, by dint of a supreme effort, they manage to topple over an object or bump into a piece of furniture, hoping in this way to attract attention. But no one understands, no one dares to understand, the message. Then comes the day when they realize that they're slowly being forgotten, that their memory is hardly ever evoked. So, sadly, they travel to the kingdom of the dead and resign themselves, at last, to drinking the waters of the Lethe. Afterward, wandering the Elysian Fields, they sometimes stop in their tracks, troubled by the vague and confused memory of a vanished past. This occurs each time a friend or loved one thinks of them.

One of the most difficult experiences after a funeral is to watch the house empty itself after having been full of people. Then one is no longer borne up by the talk of others and is left to talk with oneself.

A week after the death of his mother, Abdallah was seated in the room where she breathed her last (this, at least, is what he had been told, since at the time he was thousands of kilometers away). Cold and melancholy verses came to his mind, in which a dead woman addresses a mysteriously silent poet. It was evening, the house was sunk in shadows, but a light was on in the kitchen. There was a sudden noise—a glass falling in the dish rack. Abdallah knew then that he could never believe in his mother's death. It wasn't true. She would reappear, emerge from the kitchen, approach him with short steps, and then, leaning against the doorframe, look at him with her sad, tired eyes.

One finds the paradigmatic, archetypical mother in the story of Aladdin. Let's forget, for a moment, the Maghrebi magician, the djinn of the ring, the Chinese princess, the palace built in one night; let's even forget the famous lamp, and think instead about the figure of the mother, threading wool, earning just enough to feed herself and her son, a young rascal who cares for nothing but playing in the alleyways and getting debauched. He was so degenerate that his father, having despaired of setting him aright, died of regret. And yet—an unpleasant fact—the magic lamp is bequeathed to him!

Why him? Because his mother loved him unconditionally. No matter what he did, he was right; he was forgiven and blessed in advance. Everything he touched was a success. He felt himself carried aloft each moment by this maternal love, from which he drew a strength capable of changing the world. Did he love his mother? He never asked himself this question, lost as he was in fantasies of ambition and glory, always on the move, charging straight ahead like a madman. His mother, who disagreed with almost everything he did, nevertheless acceded to his needs and helped him achieve the most improbable, outlandish projects. He was always unaware: his mother was there to help and serve him in the same way that the air was there for him to breathe and the sun to light up his way. What she did was only what he deserved and he never felt indebted for any of it. On the contrary, he acted as if it was she who was indebted to him. Nor did she think otherwise. She had received her reward the day she brought him into the world. The only recognition she required was for him to exist, to move in front of her eyes, to be always there. Nothing more.

An Austrian writer, Josef Popper-Lynkeus, understood the tale of Aladdin as a hymn to maternal love and imagined a sequel to the story. Returning from a voyage, Aladdin learns that his mother has recently died. He begins to weep. But she, although already dead, decides "to pretend to be alive" so that he won't suffer. "And so when she heard Aladdin, who had arrived and was sobbing in front of the house, she gathered all the force of her love and lifted off the lacy shroud used to cover her body. She turned her face toward the door where her child would enter and, with an effort that no human or angel was ever capable of making, forced herself to smile affectionately as if there was nothing wrong, as if rejoicing at the arrival of her son."

But Popper omitted to ask one question, namely, what became of Aladdin after his mother's death? Many answers are possible but the most plausible may be this one, that with the funeral ceremonies complete, the son, disconsolate, picks up the lamp and rubs it, though no djinn rises before him. He tries again and again without success, and at last understands that his mother was his djinn, his magic lamp.

The Blooming Garden

ABDALLAH HADN'T SET FOOT in the medina for many years. He believed the place no longer belonged to him. He'd lived a large part of his life there, it's true, but that was ancient history, a still pool he had no wish to dive back into. His sole link with the medina was the home of his grandfather—a ruin, for all he knew, since its abandonment. The idea had always been to sell the house, but the many inheritors couldn't come to an understanding. They hesitated, delayed, and then when they were finally decided some quarrel never failed to erupt and they would have to start over again. One day, however, everyone had agreed to the sale, and so it was that Abdallah entered the medina, not by the main gate but by a very small one, close to the parking lot where he left his car.

As soon as he was a step or two inside, he felt the gate shut behind him. Protected by its walls, the medina is a closed space. Once inside, you've turned your back on the exterior world and any attempt to return is in vain. No longer visible, that world is utterly lost. Abdallah was gripped by an uncanny sensation. He didn't recognize anyone and yet the medina hadn't changed at all. Well, yes it had—the streets seemed narrower to him, the houses smaller, the distances shorter. This space, shrunken as it now seemed, nevertheless opened into a confusion of little streets and dead ends with unfamiliar names. Next to the imposing entrances of some houses there were others—low to the ground, miniscule—that seemed designed for dwarves.

What was bound to happen, happened: Abdallah got lost. A child of the medina, he was no longer able to find his way in what seemed like a labyrinth with no exit, a place he was in danger of wandering forever. He discovered there were entire sections of the medina where he was a stranger. For years he had never left the borders of his own neighborhood, running errands to the same grocer, carrying bread to the same oven, going to the same hammam and the same Quranic school. Gripped by panic, he prepared himself to ask directions from a passerby when he saw a doorway he recognized. He was sure that here was the house of Aunt Saadia.

Saadia: Lucky Woman. On holidays, Abdallah accompanied his grandfather while the old man, rapping the ground with his cane, visited his three daughters. The first visit was to Rabia (Spring), who lived the furthest away. Was this her privilege because she had the most children? The next turn went to Zohra (Flower? Venus?), where Abdallah's grandfather didn't stay long as he held her husband in utter contempt. Saving the best for last, he finished with Saadia, the oldest daughter, so close to his heart. Close to Abdallah's heart as well. Saadia distinguished herself from her sisters by serving two kinds of cake and also offered—height of refinement—not tea, but milk.

A well-read man, Abdallah was now overwhelmed with literary sentiments. Whether he liked it or not, he was an heir of the classical Arab poet, who, bent over the remnants of a campsite abandoned in the middle of the desert, brings back to life, on a current of memories, an entire vanished past ...

A small square, a public fountain. Abdallah had avoided the street where M. lived.

Every morning M. would leave home and head slowly toward the fountain, where he performed a rather strange sacrifice. Dressed simply, in loose-fitting pants and a white vest, he held a trap in which three or four rats were wriggling. Opening the faucet, he plunged his trap into the fountain and, waiting until the rats had breathed their last, chatted calmly with the Berber grocer. His lived alone, in a large house. Alone? An army of rats kept him company and his sole occupation was making war on them.

One very hot night, M. had dreamed that he was feverish and that his mother was sponging his face with a damp cloth while at the same time she brought a pair of scissors closer and closer to his eyes. He was frightened and woke up covered in sweat. A thin, flickering tongue licked at his face. If he moved his head the rat would surely bite him. He lay still for a moment, then lifted one leg and let it fall back on the mattress, causing the rat to flee. The day following this horrific night, he bought himself a rattrap.

One morning, M. failed to reappear. The grocer became worried and went to knock on his door. Receiving no response, he alerted the brother, who lived on the other side of the medina. When they finally broke into the house, they saw the rats had already begun gnawing at the door to the room where M.'s cadaver lay. In the courtyard, the rattrap was empty.

No longer required to pay their daily tithe to M., the rats lived a life of ease in the enormous home where no one now disputed their right to the property. Passersby instinctively moved away from the front door, imagining the horrors that must be taking place inside: an incessant, filthy scrabbling, scenes of orgy and carnage.

Not far from this nightmarish place, Habiba's domain stretched over a few hundred square meters. Contrary to what was suggested by the name (Beloved Woman), Habiba was a male cat, whose extraordinary feats earned him the respect of all the neighborhood children. In the morning, at precisely ten o'clock, he would leave R.'s house and begin with a leisurely inspection of his territory, making sure all was well. Next he stationed himself at the mouth of the drainage pipe and became stock-still. So as not to disturb him we positioned ourselves at a distance and tried not to breathe. All at once he plunged his left paw into the pipe and drew out a struggling rat, which, a few moments later, stopped struggling. But the kill wasn't enough for Habiba. He had to show off his prey, proclaim his triumph, receive our acclamations. Once satisfied, he returned to his stake-out until 12:30, which was mealtime. We escorted him as he trotted back home, where we witnessed a second even more astonishing spectacle. For he neither meowed nor scratched at the door to be let in; instead, gathering his forces, he leapt up and lifted the doorknocker, which then fell back with a loud clatter. Immediately, the wife of R., who always lay in wait behind the door, opened it for him and welcomed him inside with tender words. Sure of his route, he headed straight for the kitchen.

In mating season, he sometimes disappeared for days or weeks at a time. Then everyone regretted his absence. Rats would parade openly in the streets and slip into our homes. It was always a woman who, in the middle of doing some housework, came nose-to-nose with one of these crea-tures that fixed her with a livid eye. Giving a little shriek, she immediately fled the kitchen, her kingdom, and sought refuge in the room where her husband was peacefully en-sconced. He would receive her news with the same terror experienced by the passengers of a galleon who spy on the horizon the black flag of a pirate ship.

The man would begin by blaming the woman. If only she had made sure, as he was always reminding her, that the front door was always closed, this annoyance would never have arisen ... But he knows he must act, and without delay. His authority is at stake: either he dispatches the invader or he will be scorned by his wife and children and become the laughingstock of his neighbors. Overcoming his revulsion, he gets up, grabs a cudgel and rushes bravely into the kitchen, that strange, shadowy, feminine place where he almost never sets foot. With the tip of his stick he explores the corners of the room and all the possible hiding places. The rat eventually leaps forth and a Homeric combat ensues among the ovens, cooking pots, cauldrons, and dishware. The man knows he has to crush his enemy's head and that he can't leave until this task is accomplished. Finally, under the admiring eyes of his children, he exits the kitchen, exhausted, hands trembling, a beaten man, as if he just had a tooth removed without anesthesia. A ridiculous victory. Yet while the combat lasted, he had the impression of fighting not against a mere rodent, but against the emissary of some unspeakable, parallel universe, against the cunning representative of infernal and satanic forces. And indeed, in a burlesque parody of the *Iliad*, bearing the interminable and unpronounceable title of *The Batrachomyomachy*, Homer didn't find it beneath him to describe the War between the Frogs and the Rats.

Grazing peacefully on these memories, Abdallah finally arrived at his childhood home. Stepping across the threshold, he experienced the same disquiet that had washed over him upon entering the medina. A traditional-style home is also

shut off from everything outside, except for the sky arch-
ing above its courtyard. Once the door is closed, all links
with the exterior are severed. One is at home with oneself,
in the intimacy of one's deepest being (which has little to
do with that busy being one parades through the streets).
To look outside, in the absence of any windows, one must
use a ladder to climb up to the roof. From there one might
observe, as far as the eye can see, other roofs, each as white
as the next, and here and there a patch of blue sea.

The home that was so large in his memory now seemed
very small. He made a quick tour while awaiting the arrival of his cousins, who would no doubt be accompanied
by their children, and even by their children's children—a
whole tribe, whose members he saw only intermittently, at
funerals. (Death, far from separating, brings together).

He was in the house of the dead, and it seemed to him
that the ghosts of his dear ones formed a circle around him,
making one last supplication. He reproached himself for
not having visited their tombs in so many years.

He also reproached himself for not having taken care to
preserve his grandfather's books—a great store of books
that, immediately after the death of their owner, had been
stacked in wooden boxes and shut up in a room off the
courtyard, piled up together with sacks of wheat and jars of
oil, honey, and butter. They were large books, each contain-
ing in its margins another book, which commented on the
first or was related to it in some fashion. Books with dense
type, without paragraphs, indentations, or punctuation.

Labyrinthine books you entered at the beginning and didn't exit until the end, panting and short of breath, having fought past millions of letters.

Abdelmalek's library was no doubt composed in large part of commentaries on the Quran, collections of the Prophet's sayings, and theological and jurisprudential treatises. He had liked to repeat that Abdallah would become an 'alim, a scholar versed in the religious sciences. He had hoped in this way to reproduce himself, to survive through his grandson (and perhaps he had also wished, in his heart of hearts—to make this reincarnation perfect—that the frail child who accompanied him to the mosque had been named Abdelmalek). In his eyes, only the religious Law was worth dedicating one's life to, and only those books that explained the divine Word were worthy of being read. Toward the end of his life, he read nothing but the Quran.

Abdelmalek's library wouldn't have included a single work of literature. Poetry and belletrist prose held no appeal for him—for the believer, they were useful neither in this world nor the next. He was certainly aware that there had been, in the past, great poets: Abu Nuwas, al-Buhturi, al-Mutanabbi. But none of them provided a model to be followed. Who were they, after all, but drunkards, perverts, miscreants, beggars, and parasites? The few poems he did know (and which he copied out by hand), were written in praise of God and the Prophet. These poems were artistically weak and inelegant, but graced by the humble tones of those who wrote them—poor creatures who sought only to please their Creator.

How had he arrived at this aversion, or indifference, toward poetry? What teacher pushed him away from it? In the first place, there is the Quranic anathema: "And the poets—the tempters follow them. Do you not see how they wander in every valley, / Boasting of things they have not done?" The Quran does make an exception for those poets "who believe and do good deeds, Who mention the name of God often." But can such poets really write poems—good poems? A philologist of the eighth century, al-Asma'i, claimed that poetry became weak when it betrayed its essence, the batil, i.e., "lying and imposture." An awful claim, yet one that was never refuted. The ancient critics of poetry, no matter their stripe or school, had little regard for poetry based on worthy sentiments. The great Arab poets were monsters.

For Abdelmalek, all the world's poetry was contained in the little garden he built at the back of the courtyard, where he cultivated roses. In the evening, he would sit in front of the flowers and ponder, in melancholy fashion, their brief existences, the ephemeral nature of all life, the vanity of this world. Perhaps he imagined the next life as an immense rose garden where he would stroll at leisure, pausing every so often to straighten out a flower or remove a harmful weed (supposing such things still existed in paradise).

Woe to him who dared approach too close to the garden. Um Hani watched over it with perfect vigilance, fearing her husband's infrequent but terrible rages. Every so often, however, the devil would convince one of her grand-children to snip off a rose. During a moment of acute panic, she would run to find her glasses (which no optometrist had prescribed for her), arrange them on her nose, and then, with a needle and thread, re-stitch the rose and so put paradise back together.

ABDELFATTAH KILITO was born in 1945, in Rabat, Morocco. Currently Professor of Literature at Mohammed V University, he has also taught at the Sorbonne, the Collège de France, Princeton, and Harvard. Kilito has written many works of criticism on classical Arabic literature, in French and in Arabic, as well as two other works of fiction, *En quête* and *Dites-moi le songe*.

ROBYN CRESWELL is a critic and translator living in New York City. His writings have appeared in *Harper's, n+1, London Review of Books,* and *The Nation*.

WITHDRAWN

SE...
LIBRARIES
KING CAMPUS